The short story may be the most difficult of all fictional genres. In *The Bull and Other Stories*, Michael Fine, already a writer of great distinction, demonstrates he is a master. From first sentence to last, this collection is a rare delight.

—G. Wayne Miller, Author and Providence Journal reporter

"The Bull and Other Stories, rhythmic with a jazz cadence, poignant ,timely and timeless, vivid detail but above all Michael Fine is a storyteller and a damn good one at that."

—Bert Crenca, Artist, Founder of AS220

"Michael Fine's short stories rivet our readers in his monthly Sunday morning columns. We can imagine them sitting there with their morning coffee pondering the obvious and the not so obvious life dramas that Michael writes that capture you from the beginning, to the very end."

—Nancy Thomas, President of Tapestry Communications; Co-Founder and Editor RINewsToday.com

"This collection of stories takes hold and won't let go. The characters-including the bull and the oak tree - speak to the reader; you *feel* them. Lives are unvarnished - sad, banal, hopeful, sometimes all at once. Overwhelmingly real. Superb!"

—Peter Nerohna, Rhode Island Attorney General

The Bull
and Other Stories

Michael Fine

31/100

In memory of Li Wenlaing, MD

12 October 1986 – 7 February 2020

Table of Contents

The Bull and Other Stories

The Bull

Whalen his grown son Kyle came into the field to tell him about the bull, Gregory Dexter, who had been daydreaming about his dead wife Sarah, kept cutting hay. He didn't put the tractor into neutral and he didn't shut it down.

It was late afternoon in September. The air was already cool, and the sky was clear but for a few clouds on the horizon which would soon catch the light of the setting sun. The sweet smell of fresh cut hay comforted both Gregory and Kyle because it was a smell like the smell of fresh-made toast, the smell of home, of order, of hope and of love.

The air was just right for a third cutting, cool and dry but with strong sun at midday. Gregory was pretty sure he'd have this cutting crimped, raked, dried, baled, and in the barn before the next rain, but you could never tell about the weather in September, despite the clear sky. You could never tell when a hurricane might move up the coast, turn inland, and ruin everything.

Truth be told, Gregory never liked someone to come into the field while he was mowing. He had a job to do. It was important that the mowing get done so the hay could dry before the rain. Gregory didn't like being disturbed in his reverie. When he sat on the tractor, Greg was in his own world, free to think his own thoughts, to live his own life. People coming into the field usually brought news of trouble, of some distraction that would bring Gregory back to the disordered world. Cutting is straightforward. You drive a tractor in straight rows. You avoid obstacles and lift the mower at the end of the field to make your turns. As long as the equipment is in good order, you do what you came to do, and everybody ought to leave you be while you are getting it done.

Kyle was a good man, but Gregory still didn't shut down the tractor as soon as he saw Kyle. He pretended not to see him and cut for half a row while Kyle was standing there, so Greg had time to prepare himself, to come back to earth, so he wouldn't sound annoyed when he and Kyle spoke.

"Bull's out," Kyle said when the tractor was shut down.

"Damn," Gregory said. "Again. Where?"

"Over to Chaney Creek Road," Kyle said. "Sheriff called me when he couldn't get you."

"Sorry you had to drive out here. Anybody hurt? Any damage done?"

"Not yet. Oh, he did bust up a couple of Artie Knowlton's fences, so you'll need to make Artie whole for those. But Artie heard the commotion and got his cows in the barn before Tester got to them, so we are alright on that score. Artie hates it when his high and mighty purebreds get bred by a grade bull and I can't say I blame him. But you know all about that."

Kyle was a good man. Patient with his father. Kind to others. Responsible but distant. He hadn't settled down yet, not really. Kyle was a mechanical engineer. He ran a high tech machine shop in town but he spent his nights in the Knoxville honky-tonks, drinking and chasing after women. Gregory had no right to expect that Kyle would stay on the farm because Gregory hadn't stayed on the farm, not while he had a family to feed and there was money to be made. But that hadn't stopped Gregory from hoping Kyle might stay with him none the less. Kyle hadn't stayed, and his sister hadn't stayed either. That's just life in America now. Nobody stays where they are put.

"I'll put the trailer on the truck and go round up that damned trouble maker," Gregory said.

"You want me to come with?" Kyle said.

"No I've got it covered," Gregory said. "Made enough trouble for you today already. I don't know why the sheriff couldn't send one of his boys instead of troubling you."

"They can't never find you, Daddy," Kyle said. "They never know where to look."

"I'm always right here someplace," Gregory said. "They just don't want to take the time to come after me. Whatever. I still need to go and chase that animal."

"You take a gun, you hear," Kyle said.

"I don't need no gun to round up any damned bull," Gregory said. "I raised him and he minds me."

"Like a thunderstorm minds the mountains," Kyle said. "You raised up a wild grade Holstein bull. Charolais cross. They are the worst of the worst and you know it. That bull is going to kill somebody one of these days. I hate that. I just don't want it to be you."

"That bull is gentle as a kitten," Gregory said. "You just got to talk to him. You got to know how to show him who's boss and he'll respect you. I'm his daddy and he knows it."

"There ain't no two-ton horned animal who is all ornery muscle that has a boss," Kyle said. "Take that gun. And don't get between him and dinner, or him and one of his ladies."

"I got this covered," Gregory said. "Everything's under control."

The bull was done and gone by the time Gregory got to Artie Knowlton's place. He had crashed through one more fence and disappeared out of Artie's corn field after trashing it up a good bit. Lucky it was September, and the corn was in and all the corn field had on it was a cover crop of green manure. Artie was throwing up temporary fence. Artie knew Gregory was good for the repairs. They had been there together before.

Then Gregory drove north towards Clinch Mountain, where the ground was rough and the farms more spread out, the fences rougher and the tobacco patches tiny because there was no bottomland. Gregory figured Tester would go away from people, where there weren't so many fences and so much noise.

The empty trailer rattled behind Gregory's pickup. There's never any pleasure in pulling a trailer, even once you learn how to back the damned thing up, but the empty trailer felt unstable, free to bounce and sway in the wind, like it was going to skid across the road whenever the truck turned.

Gregory raised Tester from nothing. It was a stupid, self-indulgent thing to do. Gregory knew better than anyone that you don't keep an animal that don't have a use, that isn't for meat or for breeding, so there was no accounting for this choice. Selfishness on Gregory's part, that's all it was. The bull calf was three weeks old and not a hundred pounds when Gregory saw him at the auction, an ugly grade animal that needed bottle feeding for another couple of weeks and that no one wanted, and he gave twenty-five dollars for the calf before thinking it through. Gregory was alone in the house then, and feeding that calf might give him something to do. Feed him up now, leave him graze for eighteen months and then take him back to the slaughter auction. I'll get my money back, Gregory thought. No profit in it but hell, let the beast live an extra couple of months, see a winter and a summer and be a little company for me.

Amazing how you can lose a two-ton animal, how looking for the biggest bull anybody knew was still like looking for a needle in the proverbial haystack. The earth is bigger than us, Greg thought as he drove the Clinch Mountain road up beyond Camelot, looking for evidence that Tester was there, looking for a place where something very big had crashed through the bushes or for a newly busted up fence. This world is so big, so complex. You don't think about the bigness when you sit in one place, when you know every rock and every gulley in a field, and study the weather and know how the rain will run off when it comes off the roof and how the wind rattles the big barn door at night.

Gregory should have castrated Tester as soon as he brought him home. Easy enough to do. You just got to wait until the balls drop. Then you put the calf in a squeeze chute and lock the side walls around his neck so you hold him still. Then you grab the balls and pull them down, make a quick cut with a scalpel or even a buck-knife, band the vessels and the Vas, cut below the bands and you're done. You drop the calf's testicles into the hay for the barn cats to get and the calf is as good as new, the balls glistening in the hay and the calf is a steer instead of a bull you can't control.

Gregory should have just done the deed the moment Tester was off the bottle. Once upon a time, Gregory would line up twelve or twenty of the spring crop of calves and castrate them of a morning, one after the next, back when he was running a hundred or two head, before he took that job in town teaching. But that was years ago. With only one calf, it's hard to get yourself motivated, so Gregory kept putting it off, and then one day Tester was too damn big to castrate, and then ten minutes later Tester had become the biggest damn bull in Hawkins County, the biggest bull anybody had ever seen.

It was Linc Adams, one of the sheriff's deputies, who found Gregory on the Clinch Mountain road. Linc came at him at high speed, lights flashing but no siren, and just rolled his window down when his cruiser and the truck were abreast.

"Damn animal is on 11W," Linc said.

"How'd you find me?" Gregory said.

"Modern technology," Linc said. "Tracked you through your cell phone when Kyle said you weren't on the farm and Artie Knowlton said you'd been there and gone."

"Why the hell didn't you just call the cell phone then?" Gregory said.

"Kyle called, and the Sheriff called, and I called," Linc said, "but you didn't pick up."

Gregory pulled the cell phone out of his top pocket and sure enough there were four missed calls. He had the ringer off.

"Damn," Gregory said. "Sorry for your trouble."

"No trouble. That's my job. But come and collect that bull now, you hear?"

The bull was in a little field next to a liquor store on 11W, and on the other side were a mess of tract houses that Billy Testerman had built on a hillside just out of town. Tract houses and little McMansions, all running together. You could see that man-made lake from some of them houses, and Gregory reckoned that people bought there because of what they told themselves was a water-view, but it was just a view of the man-made lake which was half empty now after a pretty dry summer, though it would fill in the winter months with the rain and the snow melt and whatnot.

Kyle's truck was in the parking lot of the liquor store as was the Sheriff's cruiser and four or five other cars and trucks. You'd think none of these people had ever seen a bull before. You'd think people in Hawkins County would have something better to do than sit there and stare at some damn bull, even if he was the biggest bull anybody had ever seen.

The Sheriff was thin and shifty-eyed, and his damn uniform was too big for him. Gregory remembered him as a scrawny ten year old with freckles on the playground in the schoolyard, a kid who was a poor excuse for a wannabe bully, who spat and swore before his time, and was always getting beat on by boys older than he was and quicker with their words, their fists and their judgment of him.

"Got to move that animal," the Sheriff said.

"I didn't come just to spectate," Gregory said, looking at the little crowd who had gathered to look at Tester. "What say you move them groupies to some other part of the state."

"It's a free country," the Sheriff said. 'People will stand where people stand. They got them a show to watch. Can't say anything's more entertaining this time of day than to see you suck up to some damned animal."

"Don't want anyone hurt, that's all," Gregory said.

"I done warned them all," the Sheriff said. "Sort of like reading people their Miranda rights. You say your piece, and then you just let people who don't know their asses from a hole in the wall fail to move out of harm's way."

Gregory turned to the bull. The sun was low on the horizon and the light was red and long, and made all the colors of the field and the grass growing there, green and brown at the top, look intensely green and brown, and made the tan skin on the people watching and their blue and yellow tee shirts and trousers and stupid sundresses intensely blue and yellow, and made their skin warm tan and brown and white and somehow also deep and wise, though they were no smarter than they had all been two hours before, and were maybe considerably less smart because there they were, standing next to a field that held an unfenced and untamed two-ton bull who was all muscle and who could make a mess of trouble if he got riled or just got a dander up.

He was a great bull to see, Tester was, standing and grazing in the green field, even with those damned tract houses in the background. The only sound Gregory heard was the sound of cars and trucks whizzing and grinding past on 11W, although Gregory imagined he could hear the sound of Tester's breathing, the big, slow resonant breaths of an ocean of air moving in and out of that great, proud chest. Tester was white and tan and was a veritable mountain of muscle, which rippled over his shoulders and across a chest that was as big and rock solid as a freight train. Tester's black-tipped tail flicked back and forth in the early evening light, even though there weren't any flies now -- the beast's way of saying he would do and could do anything he wanted to. In the yard of one of the tract houses just beyond the field Gregory saw a little green and yellow and blue plastic tricycle, lying on its side beneath a swing set, and a three or four-year-old trying to right the tricycle as the child's mother called her in for dinner.

There was a brass ring in Tester's nose, which didn't do Gregory any good right then because the damned bull was loose so Gregory couldn't lead with it, and Tester's eyes were big and white and dark green with a big black pupil, and those eyes showed Tester's wildness in the way they looked away from you and even through you at the same time as they were taking you in. The world to Tester was just a set of obstacles to plow through, just a set of objectives to be achieved, and there was nothing in the world the animal recognized as meaningful or loved.

At least Tester wore a halter, which was a deep blue, and had a ring under his head where Gregory could snap on a lead rope when the beast was caught.

Gregory went to the back of the trailer, dropped the entry ramp, and pulled a stout lead rope that had a huge metal snap at one end out of a bin.

Then he walked into the field.

The big bull just kept his head down and continued grazing although Gregory knew that Tester saw him and smelled him. Tester had curved yellow-brown horns with black tips that were a foot or so long, but the horns weren't the part of him that was most fearsome. The fearsome part was the size and strength of the bull, the force he could deliver when he ran at something, shaking the ground as he charged forward. When Gregory got closer, he could hear the animal breathe, and Tester began to snort as Gregory came closer yet, small snorts that seemed to come from the back of Tester's throat like snoring or the sound a man's nose and throat makes when he is in the throes of his passion with a woman. Gregory knew Tester's sounds. Those sounds were the way he and Tester talked to one another. This was Tester saying he knew Gregory was there, and knew Gregory had expectations of him but that he wasn't ready to pay attention or homage yet and do what Gregory wanted him to do, although he also knew that Gregory was the boss-man.

Gregory stopped and stood still when he was, now thirty paces off.

"I'm ready, cow," Gregory said. "Supper time. Time for you to take a ride with me and come on home."

Tester kept grazing. He grabbed a mouthful of grass at a time in his teeth and jerked it free with a slight twist of his head at the neck and chewed and swallowed as he did so, all at the same time. It was hard to believe that this mountain of muscle and flesh could have been created out of grass alone and was maintained by it.

"Easy does it," Gregory said. You never walk up on an animal without talking. You always want the animal to know that you are there and how you are feeling and you tell them that by the sound of your voice. You talk clear but quiet, in a monotone, so as not to arouse them, and you let your voice say that you are there to help and guide them, not to attack or hurt them but that you are in charge. Bovines and horses don't see very well because their eyes are on either side of their heads so they see you with one eye at a time, in one dimension, and most of what they think and most of what they know, to the extent that they either think or know, comes from what they hear and smell and feel. Gregory knew that Tester could feel his footsteps as vibration in the ground that Tester felt in his hooves and legs, so Gregory walked deliberately, one step after the next, slowly but surely, with knowledge and confidence. Tester raised his head up, turned to look at Gregory and then Tester trotted off a few feet so he was further away from Gregory than he was when Gregory started talking to him the first time.

That's okay, Gregory thought. This is how we play this game. At home, it might take fifteen or twenty minutes for Gregory to catch the bull, fifteen or twenty minutes of getting closer and having Tester scamper a little away, of Gregory talking and waiting or turning his back from time to time to stir Tester's curiosity, before Tester let Gregory walk up to him, or before Tester came up to Gregory and nuzzled him from behind.

But home was in a small field with world class fences that Tester had tried and failed to wreck or burst through, most of the time. Gregory had put too many hours and thousands of dollars into building those fences and still there were days that Tester got out, like today. Out here, in a different field, one that wasn't really fenced with all those people watching and those cars gathered about, who knew how the bull would react?

It's hard to say you love an animal, and even harder to think it. This beast was just a beast. Tester ate grass as fast as the grass would grow. He ate and he shat and he grew. He made work for Gregory – fencing and bringing hay in to over-winter him, chasing him down when he got free. Tester chased after cows and tried to breed anything and everything in heat for five miles around, which was just a nuisance, no two ways about it, though you had to admire the bull's endless energy and resolve.

But for all his work, Gregory got nothing back. This wasn't a dog that would follow you around and nuzzle you; and it wasn't a sheep that came in for feeding the moment you came on the field, that would stand patient, watching you whenever you were in sight; it sure as hell wasn't a child that would love you back in its way, close when it was young and then from a distance as he or she aged, reflecting back your distances and your estrangement from yourself; and it sure as hell wasn't a woman, always testing you and challenging you and loving you for all your imperfections nonetheless. It was a bull, just a damned grade Charolais-Holstein cross bull that Gregory had raised up from a calf, and while there was much to admire about the beast, there sure wasn't anything to love. And yet Gregory loved that bull anyway, loved him like a son or maybe with greater love than that. Maybe it was the monstrosity of the bull. Maybe it was that Tester was unknowable, and at the end of the day maybe Gregory loved the fact that the bull could never really be bossed.

Gregory took a few steps closer, talking as he walked.

"Hold on there son," Gregory said. "I'm coming to take you home. Dinner's on the table. We'll take you home. We'll get you fed."

The bull seemed to quiet with Gregory's voice. The bull's backside was toward him, the tail flicking from side to side compulsively and sometimes rising in the air as Gregory came closer, and the bull's ears stood up at attention, rigid and twitching. The bull's great big balls were there, hanging, the balls Gregory should have whisked away as soon as he brought the calf home, but Gregory didn't notice those balls anymore, except as a reminder of this as one more among many failures.

But there was some kind of magic circle around Tester. As soon as Gregory got to within a certain distance, Tester eyed him and ran off, this time raising his head as he ran, that great white and tan head a massive countenance of stone, the neck as thick as the twisted steel cable that held up bridges, the ground shaking a little with each step. The beast shook his muzzle and snorted. Spittle and mucus came from his great nostrils and dripped from his mouth.

This time he ran further from Gregory, away from the little crowd that had gathered in the parking lot of the liquor store. He ran closer to the tract houses.

The small child, playing under the swing set, called out.

It's hard to know how an animal sees the world. We think children look like dogs to horses and bovines because children stand below the level of the animal's eyes and children are rapidly moving things, and look like dogs, wolves, jackals, and even prides of lions in the race-memory of four-footed grazing beasts. A child usually has to be within a few feet of an animal to excite its anger and its fear, but then again animals, particularly big animals, are unpredictable. Tester snorted again, a big, angry snort, and lowered his head and his eyes rolled back and his ears dropped against head so he looked more like a shark than a bull.

The ground shook. Tester started to run.

There was a rusted barbed-wire fence at the far end of the field between Tester and the child, but that fence had absolutely no meaning to Tester.

"Goddamn it bull, you get your ass in that truck now," Gregory yelled. The bull took one more great stride. Gregory looked up and saw the child getting back on the tricycle and the bull charging. Then the bull wheeled around.

It's hard to imagine how a two-ton animal can turn on a dime, but there are few forces in nature as terrible as an enraged bull and few machines of flesh as muscled and as precise that also have tremendous bulk. He listened, Gregory thought as Tester twisted in midair, as if he were trying to throw off a hapless cowboy. Goddamn it, he heard me.

Tester came around and didn't charge the child. But he also didn't stop. He responds to the sound of my voice, Gregory thought, before he saw or thought about what would come next. Get that child into the house, Gregory thought. Get that child in the house now. There's a mad bull loose, Gregory said to himself, and with that thought, he realized the extent and the enormity of the problem he had on his hands, the problem he himself had created.

Tester charged. For a moment Gregory thought Tester was coming at *him*, but that had never happened before, and Gregory thought, that would never happen. Gregory was self to Tester. Gregory was food and shelter and love, not that Tester ever felt love. It was impossible for Gregory to be danger and fear and the other.

Even so, Gregory shrank back as the bull's hooves hammered the earth and the ground shook and the bull charged the crowd of onlookers.

You don't like to hear the sound of people shouting and screaming as they scatter but that is what people do, and all that noise did was make things worse, from the perspective of an animal like Tester. Race memory again. The hunting cries of native people as they gather with lances and with spears to bring down animals many times their size for food.

Gregory saw the bull change direction. He ran toward the people and the cars as the bull bore down.

Tester came at the crowd at full speed. People cried out and scattered. No one was hurt with the first charge, thanks god, but the bull's shoulder hit one of the parked cars and flipped it on its side as he thundered through. The bull stopped in the parking lot and spun around, raising a cloud of dust. He exhaled a cloud of hot mist from his endless chest through those broad, flared nostrils. Then he trotted back through the vehicles toward the field as if he owned it. People scattered again, but Gregory knew this was a victory lap for Tester, his way of saying that he owned them. The problem wasn't that the bull was in among the people. The problem was that now Gregory couldn't tell what the bull was going to do next.

Then Tester put his head down in the field and started to graze again.

Kyle was standing with the Sheriff and they were talking.

"You got any more tricks up your sleeve?" the Sheriff said.

"He'll come around," Gregory said. "I'll get him in the trailer and we'll get him out of here."

"I don't want any of these here people getting hurt," the Sheriff said. "Seems like we got some damage already."

"You do your job and chase these people, and no one gets hurt," Gregory said. "There's no problem if all we got is a bull in a field."

"Free country, like I said before," the Sheriff said. "Seems like we got us reckless endangerment already." The Sheriff was smoking a cigarette next to his cruiser, which was white and had a broad green stripe on the side and slanted white letters.

There are two kinds of people in this world, Gregory thought. Those who do. And those who destroy, make life difficult, create damage, and then feed on the wreckage. Sabotage then scavenge. Men who can't make and can't build, but can only live off the labor of others. Parasites. Gregory knew who the Sheriff was. Always was. Now is. Always will be. People mean different things when they say loyalty and freedom.

Tester raised his head again. He was eyeing the crowd, which had re-formed.

"Hey bull," yelled some stupid scrawny kid with a buzz cut and a torn tee-shirt. Once upon a time, all the town's young men worked on a farm or in a grain elevator or for the auction or at the Co-op. Now those young men just hung around, drove hopped-up cars from place to place and got high on crystal meth.

"Okay, let's make this work," Gregory said, although he knew that stupid kid bothered him more than the kid bothered the bull. To Tester, some kid yelling was just one more insignificant human voice, and all human voices sounded alike. Except, perhaps, Gregory's voice.

Tester trotted towards them.

"Now we're talking," Gregory said, as people scattered. The bull was trotting, not charging. He was just exerting control. Marking his domain. His ears were erect and twitching and his eyes were taking it all in, not rolled back. You got to know how to read a bull, Gregory thought, although the people around him were terrified and moved behind their cars and pickup trucks. The kid with the buzz cut climbed onto the bed of his pickup where he thought he was out of harm's way.

Gregory held out a flat hand, palm up and outstretched, and walked toward Tester.

At this point in the game, Tester knew to come and nuzzle the hand, so Gregory could reach around with his other hand and snap the lead onto the bull's halter.

But Tester danced away, a few side steps, moving with so much dexterity you would have thought the damn bull was standing on his toes. Even though he didn't have toes.

Then Kyle came up behind Greg.

"Daddy, it's time to put the bull down," Kyle said.

"What?" Gregory said. "Are you crazy? This bull is calming right down. There's no harm done. I am about to put a lead on him and load him into that trailer yonder and drive him home. Mind your own business, son."

"This is my business," Kyle said. "This is everybody's business. You let this bull keep on getting loose and sooner or later someone's going to get hurt. Bad hurt."

"Nobody's getting hurt," Gregory said. "Unless you count the hurt feelings of good ole Mr. Sheriff, who can't seem to control a crowd and is getting made a fool out of by a damned animal, given that Tester is clearly the one in charge here."

"Daddy, did you bring the thirty-eight like I told you to?" Kyle said.

"Are you nuts?" Gregory said. "You don't bring a hunting rifle to corral a loose bull. Too many damned guns in this crazy country as it is."

"Thought so," Kyle said. "Daddy you just don't seem to realize how much trouble we are in here. People are tired of you and your bull getting out and wrecking their fences. Everybody's afraid of you, so no one is talking truth. You were the goddamn school principal once, and no one has the balls to cross you. But that is the truth. People hate this bull. And they think you are a fool for keeping him."

"He's just an animal," Gregory said "And a beautiful animal at that. No better example of manhood in America. And he's a beast, not a man. What does that say about the rest of us?"

"Sheriff's got a gun he'll lend you," Kyle said. "Bolt action .308. They've got all kinds of weaponry these days, surplus from Iraq and Afghanistan. What say you take care of things right here and now?"

As if he knew they were talking about him, Tester raised his great head and slowly turned it toward them, trying to pick Gregory out of the crowd. Tester was standing in the bright dying red and yellow sunlight, his amazing rippled white and yellow beauty set against the high green grass. At this point in the game Gregory was supposed to come after Tester again so Tester could run off once or twice more.

"I don't need no gun," Gregory said. "Let me go snap a lead on the beast and load him up. This silliness has gone on long enough."

Then the Sheriff closed the rear door of his cruiser. He was holding the .308, and he held the gun out to Gregory.

"You're all crazy," Gregory said. "This is a beautiful beast. He ain't hurtin' nobody. Wouldn't hurt a flea."

"I donnow," the Sheriff said. "Seems like I just saw a wild bull charge a crowd of people. Seems like there's been property damage already. Risk to life and property. Seems like reckless endangering to me."

"Daddy if you don't do it yourself, me or the sheriff's going to do this for you," Kyle said. "We just thought you'd want to clean up your own mess."

"Ain't no mess," Gregory said, but he took the gun anyway. For a man who has grown up around weapons, cradling a rifle is just a natural thing to do, like holding a baby.

"Loaded," the Sheriff said. "Safety's on, of course. The trigger is a light touch. Very smooth action for such a lethal weapon. Pretty accurate at five hundred yards. And that bull ain't but thirty yards off. "

Gregory turned the gun from side to side as if trying to recognize an object he knew but just couldn't remember. Then he shouldered the rifle and sighted through the scope, an instinct from another time, a reflex from another life.

Tester's head was high, and his ears were up. He was looking for something or someone. He wasn't angry now. Maybe a little lonely and lost, but not angry. He was looking for Gregory.

Gregory took a step forward so he was out in front of the knot of men, and he drew a bead on Tester's muzzle and then raised his sights to between Tester's eyes and then shifted his aim so that the beast's broad chest was in the middle of his sights. The skull is too thick for a reliable take down, even with a .308. The kill shot is soft tissue. You want the heart or the lungs or one of the great vessels in the neck.

Tester turned and trotted away from them again, his head high and proud, clearly the master of everything he could see. What am I thinking? Gregory said to himself. God made Tester, not man. Who am I, who are they, to think to destroy such beauty?

Gregory lowered the gun.

Then Tester turned again. He was playing. He wanted Gregory to play with him. He was ready now.

Tester saw the man he knew standing in front of cars and trucks. He was a puny thing, that man, white and thin, just an empty suit of skin hanging on a clothes line. He wasn't coming, that man, and Tester wanted him to come.

So the beast began to trot back to Gregory, to the only thing in his sight that was familiar. Tester was ready for Gregory to take him home to his own place and his own barn and his own fences.

Kyle grabbed the gun from his father and raised it.

"Somebody's got to protect us," Kyle said.

Then Kyle pulled the trigger.

When We Were Dead

We didn't know we were dead, so it wasn't a problem. They would come to visit now and then, more in the winter than in the summer because they didn't understand how we survived the cold. They thought we might die, which was more a problem for them than for us. We don't think about living or dying. We think about our feet. We are hungry sometimes. We are cold, sometimes. But our feet hurt and they weep. The yellow wet soaks our socks and the bandages around our feet. We are always tightening and loosening bandages or looking for new rags to make bandages from, so we can walk a little bit, so we can pee. It is hard to walk so it is hard to pee because there aren't places to pee nearby and the 7-11 doesn't like us coming in to pee but we do that anyway once or twice a day. They moved the train station and only let rich people in the front door so we can't go there anymore. Only we remember where the bus station used to be. That was good once. But the bus station moved away long ago too.

The snow is blue at dawn and then it becomes red and then yellow as the sun comes up and the city fills with busy people who don't see the colors we see.

We don't ever feel dead. We feel tired when we feel anything at all. We really don't even feel the cold anymore. Cold is a fact, like breathing. We fight with each other. Cold, one says. Not cold, the other says. You are bad, one says. You are a mean, lazy bitch, the other says. We know how to push each other's buttons. You think you are smart, one says. Nothing you think matters. Feelings matter, not your silly facts. Don't you get it? The other says. Are you asleep? You think the world cares that your mother loves you? Which she doesn't? And so on. That's how we pass our days. And nights. Because the dreams are just like that. Arguing. But in dreams we argue in pictures, in 3D movies of green men who come out of walls or of toothed cunts or dinosaurs or dragons that bite out our middle section, their snout between our legs that swallow us whole so we feel wet as we slither down their dark wet gullets. Tyrannosaurus Rex that lovely sexy destroyer. Whoops. Shouldn't say cunt.

A nice thin one with glasses told us we were dead. She has bug eyes behind the glasses and she smells like baby powder. She squatted next to us when she talked to us so she looked at us eye to eye, and she didn't leave us circulars. Most of them tower over us and block our light. They leave circulars they want us to read in our spare time, circulars about our rights, we think, or about food stamps or about shelters or about Jesus the savior. But you can't use circulars as bandages, and it hurts to stand and walk to the garbage to throw the circulars away so we are not littering. The thin one brought rags and sometimes bandages. It was a long time before she yielded to the temptation of the devil and asked to lock us up.

Now the lock-up, that's death. Shelter lock-up, not jail lock-up. All we ever get is shelter and that's no good because it is only for one night. First they bring you into the cinderblock building where the heat is always on. Too hot! They say take off a coat or two, take off a sweater, make yourself comfortable! But we are afraid, because without our coats and sweaters we will freeze on the street, and we need the street when the announcement comes out of the radio or out of the television or even out of an iron or a toaster, the announcement that the world is ending and that all people inside are really aliens and must be struck down. So we hold our coats and sweaters tight and then we boil so we hate inside.

And then they want you to shower. To shower we have to give up coats and sweaters and more. Same problem. Then they make you talk to a caseworker. Questions! Questions! Questions! Knives! Case workers are knives and hammers! Questions are ice picks! By then we are back home in the street. Live free or die. Then 6 AM we are free again. Whether we want to be free or not.

The thin one with glasses who brought rags and bandages was sneaky. She didn't say anything about the lockup at first. She squatted next to us. Sometimes she brought Dunkin. We love the pink glazed Dunkin. We love the vanilla cream-filled Dunkin best. No carrots or celery sticks, thank God. Carrots and celery sticks and peanut butter sandwiches, that's all the other ones bring. The thin one with glasses who didn't say a word about coming in out of the cold, about shelter or hot showers or about hot soup. All she did was wonder. I wonder about when you were born? I wonder about where you grew up? I wonder if each of you have a middle name? She snuck up on us. We didn't even know we told her because she didn't ask any questions. All she did was wonder and talk and all we did was to talk back to her.

That's how she learned we were dead. She poured her tape recorder right into a computer and the computer sliced us and diced us and told her we are dead. Our social is dead! Someone told the social that we are dead! They had killed us to steal our check. Other people get a check. Not us. No check. The street is our check. The garbage pails and the dumpsters at night are our check. Our friends on the street who give us candy and Dunkin are our check. But we have no real check, not now, not forever. If we had a check we could have Dunkin every single day. The thin one with glasses said, I wanted to find a home for you so I looked into the computer and I found that you are dead. Now, she said, we get to bring you back to life!

Who killed us? We said. No, no, no, it's all a mistake, she said. The social security made a mistake. We will help. We can fix it.

Who is we? we said. It's not broken.

Don't you want a home? she said.

We have a home, we said.

We'll do it all, she said. You'll have a roof over your head and a warm place to stay and all the Dunkin you want, every single day. All we need to do is make you undead.

You'll lock us up. You'll take away Dunkin. Social workers will come and say Dunkin makes us sick.

No lock-up, she said. You will get a place to pee.

You'll make us change undies, we said.

You'll dress yourselves. It's up to you, she said.

They'll give us pills and shots, we said. Then we won't have each other.

Only the pills and shots you want, she said. You are consenting adults.

How will you make us undead? We said. You are pretty crafty. You brought us Dunkin and snuck up on us by wondering and didn't stick us with questions so we trusted. But dead is always forever.

You'd have to come with us. To an office in Pawtucket. So they can see that you are who you say you are.

We haven't said who we are, we said. You said who we are. And who we are is dead.

But you are not dead, she said. Don't you want the world to know you are not dead?

The world doesn't care one whit about us, dead or not dead, we said. If it mattered why have they left us to live in the street since

1981? We are dead and we like it that way. We'd rather be dead than be locked up. Live free or die.

Then the crafty one came back in a white car with a woman with dark skin and frozen hair. They brought Dunkin and the woman with frozen hair also squatted. Another woman came in a green car and parked it behind the white car, both in No Parking because it is the place for buses only. The second woman brought a chair and a little box that she set up on a metal stand, and she looked at the little box, not at us, and her fingers moved on the box as if she was typing. The woman with the frozen hair tried to wonder but she wasn't good at it. Not good at it one bit. She had knives. She had the name knife. She had the birthday knife. She had the mother's and father's name knife. She had the place of birth knife.

So it came to be in the year of our Lord 2018 that we came back to the lockup. There was time – weeks or months. They brought another woman who had an orange coat and long dangly earrings which we almost grabbed who read from a paper and made us undead. Other people came. A man with a ponytail and a camera came. He took pictures from all angles – from standing and sitting and squatting and even laying on his side on the ground. The Governor or the Senator came, somebody like that, a white man and a white woman wearing camel's hair coats and scarves and shiny black leather gloves. They leaned over us and shook our hands as the man with the ponytail took pictures and they also blocked the sun but they looked very pleased with themselves, as if their mothers had just told them they were behaving and being so polite and so good.

After that things happened on their own. They brought a white minibus that had a wheelchair lift and knew how to lean over so the door was close to the ground, and it sucked us right in. The white minibus took us to the lock-up, which was a lock-up even if it wasn't locked. We changed our undies. Took showers. The water was hot and it felt so good, like Mommy, and we could feel skin which has feelings of its own, instead of wearing our crust. They brought us vanilla crème Dunkin every day. We took off the sweaters and coats, one by one. No medicines or shots though. We want to be together. Arguing but together.

It is different. Maybe we are in heaven. We sleep lying down in a bed. Not cold. Never cold. But we sit in the community room every day and watch the TV, the colors knives themselves, too bright, but we must watch them, those moving colors. They are also vanilla crème Dunkin and our eyes watch and we are there, not here.

We are not dead. We breathe, in and out, in and out, and we remember the pinks and purple blues of dawn. We remember sitting outside on our bench in the winter with no one else around, our breath coming in little clouds, our nose dripping, warm inside our crust, remembering the days and nights we were dead and so alive at once.

Bernie Sanders, Elizabeth Warren, Infantile Liberalism and the End of Democracy

Introduction

That old white man sounds righteous enough: democratic socialism, Medicare for All, college for free, and tax the rich. Tio Bernie. Not bad, on paper. And that thin white woman, that Pocahontas woman, she sounds pretty much the same, lots of big ideas and so forth, but she lectures at you like she is a school teacher, going on and on and sounding so high up and mighty. Talking about the victims. They always talk about the victims, those poor people who keep getting screwed. Like we don't know that those poor people is us. They always talk about the middle class, like the best anybody wants is average. They never talk about the love between people, about our communities, because they just can't remember that we exist and our communities exist to do way more than just to vote for them. They never talk about justice or democracy. All they ever talk about is themselves.

Trump is a problem and he needs to be gone. Everybody knows that. A racist and a schoolyard bully, who gets your goat by calling names and then will push you over one of his friends, who sneaked up behind you on hands and knees, if you ever take a swing at him. Just a liar and a cheat, but at least he doesn't take no guff from the high and mighty types, who think their stuff don't stink. And he does what he says he's going to do, even when it's bad. He doesn't hide behind promises that no one can keep. Or talk so that you can't understand what he means.

Doesn't help me much, Asoka Goh thought. I still have to make a life for myself, pay off my student loans, get a job, help my parents, look right to the community, dream some dreams, and get ahead in this crazy country. Morning to night. Seven days a week. Kids. Work. Class. Meetings. Church. Kids. Work. Class. The damn cell phone doesn't ever quit.

And their impeachment, please tell me what *that* was about. Trump is a bad hombre. We all know that. They had no chance of kicking him out from the start. We all knew that too. So what did they do it for? To hear themselves talk? To look smart to themselves? To make sure we knew they are better than we are. Trump is who we live with in the street, every day of our lives. He's not going away because you hold some hearings in Congress. And he's not going away with one little election, even if he loses and goes off to Florida, his tail between his legs. He's been here forever, and he'll be here forever, regardless of who gets elected.

They don't get that. And they don't get they are just as much him as he is. Student loans at 6 percent. You got to take a twenty thousand dollar class to be a medical assistant and make 12 bucks an hour. Otherwise you get to work in McDonalds and make 10 bucks an hour. Their high schools don't work, their colleges are a rip off, and you can't buy a two family house anymore or live any kind of life on what most of us make. Let alone afford rent. Got to work a day job, a night job and a weekend job and attend to your kids, and your family and your friends and the community. Those people suck our blood just like Trump. They make money from everything we want or need. They do the advertising and the movies and whatnot. They are the lawyers and the doctors and the schoolteachers. They know all the right answers. They make plenty of money themselves. And they protest all the way to the bank. They whine and complain like they are so much better than that asshole and everyone else to boot.

And they send all them emails, asking for money. Begging for money. You think we don't know about how that money pays the salaries of the people who send those emails, so they can just keep asking for more, talking trash about each other to get people riled up, to get people to give them more money yet? Them emails say it loud and clear: that they think they are smart and we are just dull, that we don't know how the game is played, who the players are, and who wins and who loses in the world that they made and we pay for?

She was more floozy than not, and Jack Montecalvo had no idea how she ended up in his bed or even what her name was, until he did. It took a minute, in the middle of the night, to turn the warm body next to him into a story, and so he didn't touch or rub or explore until he figured it out. And then, less floozy than not. She was a good looking woman, for 50, a teacher with a wild streak, Janine. Janine Johanson, brunette once, blond now. Brown eyes once. Brilliant blue eyes now.

They had run into one another at Spikes, a sports bar in Cranston on Super Bowl night. Loud place, too loud to think or talk. And who cared? No Patriots this year. They'd known one another a little for years. Truth be told, he always had a good feeling about her, a simpatico. She was Jimmy Johanson's sister. She had a brain and a brave wild streak that didn't care what people thought or thought of her. She'd always been out there, a question that he hadn't yet asked.

They ended up sitting next to each other, jammed close at a table with ten other people, by accident, not design. The other people were loud and everyone in the bar was loud, cheering and moaning with each play. That's what football is for. They talked, or tried to, just to catch up. You have to lean in close to talk in a bar that's loud. That, and a little alcohol, and then a little too much alcohol, opens the brain to possibilities and urges not previously experienced or, perhaps, acknowledged. The Chiefs win. You dance a little. It's a Sunday night, so you go slow because there is work the next morning. You have one or two extra to drink, in the moment. Careful now. Got to drive home. But then caution goes out the window. You feel what you feel, you want what you want, and the rest, as they say, is history.

Methods

So the black kid comes to the union hall and we have a chat. I can do that much for Janine. He's got a good story: Indian descent. Jamaican mother, Dominican father, not together, of course. Mother comes here eight months pregnant so her baby gets to be a citizen. Grows up in South Providence and the kid survives that. Goes to Blessed Sacrament and then Central High School, and survives that. Goes to CCRI and then RIC and survives *that*. Works three jobs and is looking for someone to cut him a break. Three jobs! He has a degree in counseling and is working on a Master's in Public Administration at night. One course a semester, maybe two. It will take him three years, minimum. He's some kind of peer counselor, working for a non-profit. $18 an hour and crappy health insurance with big co-pays and a $7000 deductible. He works in a group home on weekends. $12 an hour. No benefits. Nights cleaning offices. $15 an hour, no benefits, under the table. What a chump.

The good news is that he's not just an entitled poor Black kid with an attitude. He's just a poor Black kid, trying to figure out how to survive in America. I don't hear none of that white privilege, micro-aggression, Black lives matter crap. Yeah his mother was an immigrant who came here just to make her kid an American citizen. Yeah his mother lived on welfare. Yeah he grew up on food stamps, and we all paid his way. But he's just a kid, and he's hustling to make ends meet. And he has three kids of his own, somehow, and he's trying to make that work too.

So I tell him about the way it goes in the trades. About the hiring hall. About the benefits and the over-time. What real numbers look like. About all for one and one for all. You can do this, I tell him. I tell him despite myself and what's left of my better judgment. I'll take a little shit over this from this one and that one. But we'll all survive.

Results

The best thing you could say about the woman was that she was non-descript. She was thin-ish and usual, not tall, not squat, not shapely, not even really thin. Her hair was cut short and was mouse-colored – not brown, perhaps tan, not strikingly cut. It didn't get into her eyes, which you didn't notice, because she didn't look directly at people, although she also didn't look away. She wore an olive colored cloth coat and carried a large hand bag with a shoulder strap, and she came on the #4 bus. She walked off the bus carefully, holding the handrail so she wouldn't stumble or slip when she stepped onto the wet pavement, which was still slick from last night's rain and from the ice left over from the night's cold. Most of the ice had melted when the air warmed a little in the morning sun, which was bright and clear but not yet warm.

But the woman walked without hesitation toward a school where Asoka Goh was working as a union electrician, wiring a room in a wing of the school that was being renovated so there were outlets to plug in computers at each desk, and so there were state of the art smart white boards and huge video monitors on each wall, in order to give the students a twenty-first century learning experience, so they could learn visually and learn to function as part of teams. The school was in an old neighborhood of Cranston, Rhode Island. Its students were the children of people from all over the world – from Cranston itself, descended from English and Irish immigrants, who had arrived before and in the years after the civil war, who had come to be yeoman farmers or factory mill hands; they were the children of people descended from Native Americans, whose ancestors had come thousands of years before in waves across the land bridge from Asia and then fanned out over two virgin continents, and had been mostly wiped out by disease or enslaved and had shrunk themselves through intermarriage or by taking small jobs so that they were almost invisible; they were the children of people who were the descendants of slaves and freedmen from Africa who had remade themselves into Americans despite all the efforts of people of European descent to make them completely disappear – by violence, by exile, by imprisonment, by exclusion and by what was sometimes called benign neglect which was anything but benign; they were the children of people descended from Polish and Russian Jews who left the Pale of Settlement in the 1890s and worked in the junk business or the rag trade or in the mills or had little stores and saw their brothers and cousins work their way up to riches while the people who lived in Eastern Cranston, near the water, in the old houses and the old neighborhoods were left behind. They were the children of people whose families had come from Cabo Verde off the west coast of Africa in the 1850s to work as whalers out of New Bedford and Nantucket, or work in the cranberry bogs in southeast Massachusetts and then in the mills, or their cousins, from Brava and Pria who had come in the 1990s or even in 2010 directly or by way of Holland because the money was better here, because there were doctors and hospitals and schools so that coming here was a way to have a better life after all despite the cold and then snow in winter; they were the children of people from Liberia whose families had been coming here since the nineteen eighties; and they were the children of people from all over the rest of West Africa, from Mali and Nigeria and Sierra Leone; the children of people from Cambodia, both Hmong and ethnic Chinese; the children of people from Nepal and from Bhutan, of Rohingya people from Myanmar; the children of Syrian refugees from its civil war; the children of people from Puerto Rico, the Dominican Republic, Honduras, El Salvador, Mexico, Guatemala and Colombia; and a sprinkling of children of people from Brazil, Peru, and Nicaragua and other nations too numerous to count.

The woman had timed her arrival to coincide with the arrival of the students. The woman looked a little too old to be the mother of a student, but too young to be an abuela, a grandmother. The school yard was filled with students who were arriving on foot, arriving in cars, and arriving by the yellow school buses that had pulled up to the curb. The school yard rang with their energy and excitement, their teasing and singing and calling out.

It was the end of winter. There were no leaves on the trees yet but the branches of the shrubs had turned red and green and budded, and were preparing to bloom. The birds had returned and were skittering in the bushes, on the ground and amongst the naked branches of the trees overhead. A cool breeze blew in from Narragansett Bay which was just a block and a half away.

The woman walked up the steps of the school with the crowd of entering students and passed through the open school doors, almost invisible because of her ordinariness. She and the students passed in front of the school office window which had thick glass and a set of sign-in sheets for visitors. There was a school secretary who stood behind the window but she was on her cell phone and was looking away, because this parade was the same parade that walked past her every day, day in and day out, always without incident.

The woman entered through the glass front doors that are normally kept locked. She passed into the entryway and turned to the right following the crowd and headed toward the wing where Asoka Goh waited.

Asoka Goh hadn't begun work yet. He had come early and unloaded several spools of wire, a box of outlets and a second box of bright blue black and red connectors from his truck and had also brought two bright yellow ladders in from the truck and leaned them against the wall. His boss, Ricky James, hadn't yet arrived. Ricky James would show fifteen or twenty minutes late and usually walked in with the plumber on the job, a guy named Dave, and Dave's assistant. Jerry, the GC, didn't usually show until eleven and he was in and out in half an hour, though he often took longer if the work wasn't moving. More often than not Jerry would come back at two before everyone knocked off work for the day, just to check in and jerk everyone's chain.

Asoka Goh was the electrician's apprentice. He did class two nights a week and had been at it for three years so he was making pretty good money now. Everyone knew he was smart and able and was just biding his time. He was grateful for the work and for the promise of more work and a better deal as time went by. He took a bunch of crap for being an apprentice, for being young, for having done college and graduate school and still ending up like the rest of these bozos, working for a living. He took more crap yet for being an immigrant kid, for having come up in Providence and for having his kids so young, but he had a thick skin and could give as well as he could take when he had to.

But mostly Asoka just did his work and kept his mouth shut because the assholes on the job didn't mean anything to him. They were well meaning, more or less, when they weren't being stupid racists but for Asoka they were just means to an end, his pathway to a master's license. If he had been a smoker and they weren't on a school job Asoka would have had a cigarette right then, as soon as the ladders and wire were set up and ready to go.

He wanted to get started so they could finish early for once. But the rules are the rules. An apprentice can't work without the master there. So Asoka looked out the window, thought about his own kids and their mother, walking their two older ones to school in North Providence, and thought about Jasmin, who was trying her best to be a good mother but seemed like she didn't have a brain in her head half the time. He thought about all the shit he had to put up with, day in and day out, and how hard it was to keep his mouth shut because whatever he said made things worse instead of better.

The non-descript woman in the olive cloth coat walked down the hall behind two girls. They were fifth graders and tall for their age but they still only came up to the woman's shoulders. They were perfect. Just the right height.

The woman took a giant step forward, which brought her between the two girls.

She grabbed both girls at the same moment, wrapping an arm around each and covering their mouths with her open hands. Then she pulled the girls into the first open door she saw, into the new wing where Asoka Goh waited, looking out the window. She pushed the girls into the room, slammed the door behind her, and pulled a knife from a scabbard that was hanging from her waist under the olive green cloth coat. She pulled both girls to her again and held the knife against the throats of both girls, who stood, quiet and trembling, in shock and too terrified to speak.

Asoka turned to see who had slammed the door, expecting his boss, the plumber or the GC.

Instead there was a woman holding a knife at the throats of two school girls.

It took a moment for Asoka to assemble the picture in front of him and turn it into an image that had meaning. There was a woman with a knife that she was holding at the throats of two school kids. School shooting? Only a knife not a gun. Terrorist kidnapping? A plain looking white woman. What the fuck?

The woman looked at Asoka. She saw a person of color in jeans and work boots with intelligent eyes, wearing a tool belt and a white hard hat, standing next to a yellow ladder.

The school buzzer rang, signifying the beginning of the class day.

"Good morning students and teachers," a voice said, sizzling over a distant loudspeaker, distant because the speaker in the renovated wing had not been wired yet. It was a middle-aged woman's voice, self confident, a little worn but still strong and cheery.

"Today is Tuesday February 12, Abraham Lincoln's birthday. Wait," the voice said, pausing.

There were some crackling and bumping, the sound of a hand held over a microphone.

"Active shooter. Active shooter. This is not a drill," said the voice that now trembled.

"What do you want?" Asoka said.

"For you to be out of my way," said the woman holding the two girls, her voice crisp, calm and measured.

The girl on the woman's left was named Tiffany. Her parents were Guatemalan and she was undocumented but no one was supposed to know that. The girl on the woman's right was named Ashley. Her mother worked in a bank and her father was in jail but no one was supposed to know that either. She played soccer in the afternoons in the spring and the fall and liked to watch tennis on TV.

"What are you going to do?" Asoka said.

"Sacrifice the lambs and paint blood on the lintels so the Lord will pass over the houses of the just when he comes to annihilate the first born of the heathens. Oh Pharaoh! Let my people go," the woman said.

"You crazy," Asoka said.

"Not as crazy as you. Not as crazy as Sodom and Gomorrah where men and women have their way with each other in the street, where the widow and the orphan are cast out. The moneychangers are now in possession of the temple. Their computers sell children into harlotry. Mine eyes have seen the glory of the coming of the Lord!" the woman said.

She raised the knife above the throats of the terrified girls, who began to whimper, not understanding a word of what the woman said but smelling her madness.

"Wait!" Asoka said. 'What's your name?" he asked in a voice from his past, when he had been a chump but studied people and their emotions.

"Mine eyes have seen the glory of the coming of the Lord!" the woman said. She looked in Asoka's direction but she looked past him, at a voice that came from a faraway place.

Engage, said a voice in Asoka's head, a voice from something he knew or read long ago. *Enter the delusion.*

"What does the Lord call you? " Asoka said.

"The Lord calls me to do justice!" the woman said.

"With what name does the Lord call you to justice?" Asoka said. He had been good at this, once.

The woman looked at Asoka for the first time.

"I am Miriam, sister of Moses," the woman said. She looked at Asoka and looked through him at once, as though she was seeing through him and into another world.

Engage. Empathize. Options. Hard to believe any of that crap was worth anything but it was still there, stuck in the back of Asoka's brain.

"Miriam Glory to God that you are here!" Asoka said.

"Glory to God!" the woman said.

"I'm with you, girls," Asoka said. "It's all good. Tell us your names."

"They are lambs!" Miriam screamed. "Put down your staff, infidel! I know your tricks and your magic."

Asoka knelt slowly. He put his coffee cup on the floor.

"I have no staff, sister," he said. The he stood up again slowly, his eyes on the knife, with the girls between him, the woman and the knife.

Miriam was looking through Asoka again, not at him.

The hallucination had her. *Organize the ego. Now. Keep her in the present.* Otherwise the hallucination owns her and can strike like a pit viper without warning.

"Glory to God!" Asoka said.

"Glory to God in the highest!" Miriam said.

There was a siren. God alone knew what sirens, flashing lights and uniforms would do to this madwoman.

"God says let my people go!" Asoka said.

"Go down Moses!" Miriam said.

"Let my people go!" Asoka said.

"We will kill the Pascal lamb and smear the blood on the doorways of God's chosen people!" Miriam said.

A puddle formed at the feet of one of the girls.

Red and blue lights came through the window behind Asoka and washed the room.

Asoka imagined a swat team getting in position.

"Abraham! Abraham!" Asoka said, buying, now praying for time.

"Here I am!" Miriam said.

Suddenly Asoka realized that he was between the window, Miriam and the girls. He was a Black man. She was a white woman. And that this was still America. You got to play the cards you're dealt.

"Don't lay your hand on the boy! Don't do anything to him! For now I know that you are a woman who fears God, because you have not withheld your son, your only son, from me," Asoka said.

Miriam stared at Asoka for an instant, dazed.

A pinpoint of red light flicked from the wall to the yellow ladder to the arm holding the knife, and then it disappeared.

Then, without warming, as the red dot found the back of his head, Asoka dropped to his knees.

There a loud single crack, the sound of a hand slapping a face.

The knife clattered to the floor, and Miriam fell backward, twisting as she fell. The girls fell forward.

The bullet intended for Asoka hit the knife, not the girls. God is good after all.

Asoka kicked the knife across the room and covered the uninjured bodies of the girls with his own body, because this is still America, and you never know what's going to happen next.

Men and women wearing helmets and body armor poured into the room.

Maybe there is a god after all, Asoka thought.

They had Asoka and Miriam spread-eagled on the floor in one half second, and they bundled the girls out of the room. Faster than a speeding bullet. And who, dressed as a mild mannered reporter. Like the headlight on a southbound train.

Nothing much mattered after that.

Discussion

The world being what it is, it took three days for the police to figure out that Asoka was who he said he was. Just a man. Not involved. No terrorist.

Didn't take them ten seconds to figure out that Miriam, or whoever she was, was crazy as a loon. You would have thought the moment words came out of her mouth, the police would have figured out that Asoka wasn't involved at all, except for being in the wrong place at the right time, and that he had saved those little girls' lives. You would have thought they made a hero out of him. But they had to do their due diligence, and by the time those police put two and two together, the world had moved on.

Conclusion

The truth doesn't matter much. The people on television and whatnot, they have big ideas and make big promises. But they must know they can't deliver on any of it. It's just play acting, all makeup and lights, not real life.

But they want us to show up and vote anyway. For who? For what? It's about them, not us.

We are the deplorables, the disposables, the deniables. Who do they think they are fooling?

But we do get fooled again. Every single time.

A man does what he has to do, and disregards the rest. Lie la lie lie lie lie.

A Long Way To Fall

F irst came the Gypsy Moths. Then the southern pine beetle and the emerald ash borer. Then the hot dry summers. Thirteen percent of the trees died. 50,000 acres of trees. Mostly oak.

Good luck and bad luck, bundled together. Climate change, real after all. Sad to lose all those oaks. But dead trees make more work for a tree guy.

The best money in forestry is in writing forest plans, subsidized and paid for by the good old USDA. The second-best money is the clear-cutting of hardwood forests if you can find a forest where the land is flat and the forest is mature. Allan Gordon hated clear-cutting but it paid the bills. Forest plans are mostly desk work, which Allan also hated. Allan liked to be in the woods.

Clear-cutting was just wrong. He was no tree hugger, let me tell you. A man has to make a living. Still, clear-cutting bothered something in his soul. To tell the truth, dropping any tree bothered something in his soul, but it was a small bother, a whisper, not a shout. Clear cutting was a shout. Even so, you can't live on air. A man does what he's paid to do and disregards the rest.

They called him to cut a big dead oak in a ravine. Now he was standing beneath it. He came ready to climb, with his climbing harness and his green helmet, his orange and white chainsaw hung from his harness, but he sure wasn't going up *this* tree. Too damn big to get a flip-line around.

The old oak was the biggest dead tree Allan had ever been asked to drop. Old growth, near as he could make out. A hundred feet tall or more, bigger than the three other big oaks nearby. Maybe two, maybe three hundred years old. Something like eight feet in diameter at the stump. More than fifteen feet around – so big that three men holding hands couldn't reach around it. Oak grows straight up, thrusting out of the earth, a huge trunk with no branches at all until you are two-thirds of the way up, so this one was just ridged gray-brown trunk for sixty feet. Then three huge branches. Then a leafy crown. Sixty feet of climbing without a rest, without a place to secure a line. No way. Sixty feet is a very long way to fall.

The old oak was in a grove of big oak on a steep slope, on a north-facing glacial moraine a couple of hundred yards from the nearest road. The rock-strewn slope was pockmarked by big boulders and broken-off hunks of ledge that had been strewn about when the glaciers retreated, with a stream that was a waterfall in slow motion, that gurgled and sang as water came off the hillside and through the rocks.

The old oak's ridged bark made Allan think of elephant hide. The bark thickened into ridges that ran straight up and down. The grooves between the ridges were dark gray-brown, almost black, and the bark itself was warm to the touch – warmer for sure than the late October air. The tree felt old and wise. The grove of big oak reminded Allan of a herd of elephants, also old and wise, slow moving but ponderous, balanced, resilient and all-knowing.

Condos. They were going to build condos. In a rocky gorge that was good for nothing, that was too rocky and too sloped to farm and too dark, because it was north facing, to use for grazing. No one ever wanted to put a house here. No one even hunted here – the slope was too steep. There was a story about a wolf den, once, back before the settlers came. Wolves and snakes, maybe. But not good for people. The old oak had grown undisturbed for hundreds of years.

Only now some developer was going to turn this grove of old oak into condos and parking lots. They were going to bulldoze a long drive in from the road, terrace the hillside, pour foundations and build themselves a development right into this slope, just so some rich guy could make himself a bundle. Condos on both sides of the stream, which they were going to leave because it was way too expensive to divert. The stream, which once fell between the rocks in the dark glen and became a rushing waterfall after a hard rain or when the snow melted, would become scenic natural beauty, a selling point for the development that was about to take the place of a beautiful grove of old growth oak that had never been cut, had rarely been walked under by human people, and could never be replaced.

You'll never get a bucket truck up here, Allan thought. Not that any bucket truck would be of any use. The damn tree was too tall and the branches were too big to cut from below. No way to limb this tree. The damn thing would have to come down whole. A whale of a tree. Bitch and a half to drop. More dangerous than dynamite.

Allan walked around the tree. Big, really big. Bigger than it looked. Then he walked around it a second time. It wanted to fall northeast, up the slope, because the biggest branch grew in that direction, sixty feet up and itself likely three feet in diameter.

Allan mapped his escape, the first thing he did when he was getting ready to drop a tree, because you never really know how a tree is going to fall. There was another big oak about twenty yards away, but there were a couple of big rocks, thick brush and a few saplings between the big one and that one, rocks he'd have to weave around and brush he'd have to navigate if he were trying to get out of the way of a surprise fall. Pretty sketchy, as a route to safety. Hard to know how much time he'd have if the monster fell the wrong way. Hard to know how much protection another tree would give him, once this monster started to move. The fall of a twenty ton tree was like a small nuclear explosion. Once the tree leaned a little, once it started to fall and picked up speed, it would obliterate anything that lay beneath it. The earth would rock when it hit the ground. They'd hear the crash a mile away, the sound of a locomotive hitting a concrete wall. Its huge branches and any tree in its way would be splintered by the force of the fall.

He'd need a sixty inch saw to drop a tree this big, with a bar that was almost as long as Allan was tall. The bar alone cost more than most of Allan's chain-saws. It would take days to hollow out the trunk, to carve blocks of wood that were each as wide as most of the trees Allan usually dropped. Once he had it on the ground it would take most of a week to cut the trunk into slabs, split the slabs and haul them out.

You'd need a front-end loader to move those slabs and a good size dump truck to carry them away, but you'd have to carve yourself a little road just to get that equipment in, and you'd make a mess of the forest floor and that little waterfall.

If you left the damn tree alone the world wouldn't end. If you just left it, it would fall on its own eventually. It would rot from the inside the way oak does, because oak is a wet wood, and it would drop its branches one by one. It might take thirty or forty years for the tree to fall on its own. Maybe more. And then another twenty or thirty years for it to rot. No harm would come from doing nothing. Old trees died, fell and rotted for millions of years before humans came around. The world carried on very well without us, then, thank you very much.

But that was before condos.

A man has to make a living.

The tree was dead. It had to come down. There were no two ways about it. And then rest of that old oak grove with it. They were just trees. Trees grow back. Trees would grow in other places.

He bid the job. He took care to cushion his bid so there was a margin in case things didn't go as he planned, so he'd be sure to make decent money. He included three weeks of work and the cost of that long bar. A part of him hoped he wouldn't get the job. Lots of dough. He'd make plenty if the tree came down smoothly as long as he didn't get squashed like a bug in the process. He'd still likely come in under his competitor, a national tree removal operation with thousands of green trucks, a famous name in the industry, and so much overhead that Allan could usually under-price them on specialized jobs like this. Ten days to drop the big oak. A week to cut that sucker up. Allan knew trees. And the tree business, better than anyone.

Allan got the job.

One day about three weeks later Allan stood under the old oak holding his big Stihl, his best saw but boy it felt puny now compared to the size and majesty of that oak.

He started to work. First he prepared his escape route. He cut the brush and saplings nearby and moved as many rocks as he could between the old oak and its neighbor tree so there was a clear path to some protection.

Then his saw touched the bark of that tree for the first time. The tree was just wood, like any other tree. The saw sprayed a shower of tiny brown and yellow wood-chips away from the trunk, a shower of wood-chips mixed with white smoke from the saw's exhaust. The saw whined as it cut, a mechanical screech that rose and fell in pitch as Allan squeezed the trigger of the saw. The air smelled from that exhaust, the smell of burnt gasoline and thirty weight oil.

First Allan laid in a felling cut, a huge vee'd notch, on the side and in the direction that the tree would fall. That cut that took him ten hours to place because of the size of the trunk. Then Allan put on the six-foot bar and laid in a base cut, on the side away from the side of the fall, notching out slabs of wood the size of shipping cartons to create a lateral cave almost big enough to fit a man inside the trunk itself. He placed wedges as he worked, blocks of wood that could support the tree's weight, as protection, so the weight of the tree didn't shift and surprise him, so the tree would fall exactly where he planned it to drop.

It took three days to finish the base-cut. That left the trunk hollowed out, so there were just two columns of wood, one on each side, holding the weight of the trunk. Allan could see through the trunk at its base.

A strong wind could have dropped the tree at that point. The weight of the tree, shifting with the wind, would have splintered the support columns of wood, once the mass of the thing began to move. And then the whole trunk would have come down, smashing everything in its path.

While Allan worked, the developer had a bulldozer cut a dirt road in from the street, so a front end-loader and dump trucks could get to the site. The sound of machinery, of grinding gears, the whine of the chain saws, the hammering and the voices of men yelling over the noise filled the dark north-facing glen, and now the air smelled of motor oil, grease, and diesel exhaust.

It was fall. The leaves were off most of the maples, but the oak trees that were still alive held onto their leaves as they always do, dark green and brown leaves that stay waving in the wind long after most other leaves have fallen. There were slashes of red, hickories that hadn't lost all their leaves, and of yellow, birch leaves that hadn't yet dropped. The white birches could now be seen in the woods, white slashes on a gray and brown hillside, their white trunks bringing order and grace to the woods, exclamation marks against the grey and brown rocks, their yellow leaves a brilliant gold, a hint or a reminder of life everlasting, which, of course, it isn't.

Better to work in the fall when the air is cool, even though the days are shortened and the sun, low on the horizon, glints into your vision. Too damned hot, in the summer, and the long days let you work way past exhaustion, which is when you make mistakes.

When the back cut was nearly finished, Allan walked away to recheck the tree and his calculations. The weight was to one side. Gravity would put the tree where Allan wanted it. All he had to do was finish the back cut, and get out of the way. Gravity is a tree-guy's friend. As long as it's not your enemy.

There was no margin of error now.

Allan cut the first of the two support columns with an old, almost worn out Stihl, holding his breath as he cut. No reason to lose your best saw if something went wrong. They were very close now. The weight of the tree settled into the new cut, closing it. The least wind could now send the tree crashing down.

Then he placed the last cut.

He touched old Stihl to the remaining wood. His eyes were fixed on the cut he was making, and he held his breath again.

This was the moment of greatest danger. The faintest breeze might start the tree's fall, might push the tree the wrong way, crushing him. Or if he'd read the tree wrong, gravity alone might drop it a different way, on top of him, or it might twist as it fell, and Allan would be a pancake just the same. Once the tree started to move, once it started to fall, there was no turning back. Twenty tons of wood. The trunk would crush anything and everything in its path.

Then the space above his saw became a tiny bit larger than it had been. The cut he was placing opened just a millimeter. Almost undetectable. Something had changed, had moved. The tree was starting to fall.

Allan cut the saw's engine, and ran like hell.

The tree didn't sway or twist. It hesitated, wise at its tipping point.

It leaned a little, just an inch or two at first.

And then all hell broke loose.

Wood cracked and groaned. The massive tree toppled, opening a whole new sky behind it. The old oak came to earth with a whoosh and a crash and a boom, shaking the earth as if a meteor had landed, and drove the boulders that lay beneath it deep into the ground. The entire universe was sucked into the tree's fall for a moment. The air, the trees and brush beneath it, the rocks and the stream jumped and then trembled in the aftershocks.

The woods fell still.

The big oak lay on the ground, a continent on its side, an era ended.

There was light in the woods where there had been only shade. A cool breeze came up. The red leaves of a shag-bark hickory nearby that Allan hadn't noticed twisted in that breeze. Some of those leaves fluttered to the ground.

Time marches on. The old oak was on the ground, and Allan had failed to die dropping it.

Allan began to limb the tree.

He first cut the branches that were furthest out and had been highest in the sky, working back toward the trunk. The branch wood was already dried, already brittle. Dry wood is hard on chain saws. Cutting the trunk was a huge job but he had a week to do it. He'd get it done.

The sun started to set. It was red and gold and purple at the edges of the horizon.

Allan put his saws in the truck and went home.

Sad to see the old monster go. Good that that the oak came down neatly, and fell where he wanted it to fall. Good he'd survived this one without getting hurt. Ducked another bullet. Live and let live, if and when you can.

A man has to make a living.

As he fell asleep that night, Allan remembered the new light and the new sky that where the big oak had been, and the red and yellow leaves that fluttered down in this new space.

There was nothing else left to know.

The old oak was on the ground.

Allan was still alive. For another moment or two.

Anyway

He was an old white man and he was hard to like, let alone love, and she was a kid, or that's how she thought about herself, just a dumb kid most of the time but a wiseass when she wanted to be, half Dominican and half Puerto Rican, who lived with her mother and brother in a triple-decker in Pawtucket, who saw her good-for-nothing father once in a while when he got sober enough to remember that he had a daughter after all. Nineteen. Hot, she tried to tell herself, because she tried to be, like her cousins and her friends, but the truth was that she was just a kid who hadn't seen much of the world at all and only barely knew what day of the week it was. Mother on disability. Brother sixteen. You do what you got to do to keep body and soul together.

He. Mr. Lewin. An old man who just sat there like a bump on a log. He spent all day listening to records on a record player, if you can believe that. He listened to old music that was slow and fake romantic. Lots of violins. No beat, no rock, no punch – nothing alive. The old man just sat there with his eyes closed. Sometimes he sang along, sang to himself. You had to wonder what he was thinking about, what he was remembering.

And the old man wanted things. You'll bring me a cup of coffee, he'd say. You'll bring me a biscuit, he'd say, because he liked these weird old biscuits with chocolate on one side that came from

England. You'll bring me a plate of Oreos, he'd say, the only thing he liked that normal people actually eat. Never, do you mind grabbing a cup of coffee, or, how about some of those amazing cookies, or even, would you be so kind as to carry in Oreos, please, which is how they talk in the old movies Jazmin had seen. No. Just, you'll bring me this. You'll bring me that. As if that old man owned the world and Jazmin in it. As if Jazmin was a just a part of what he owned, like an arm or a leg on someone else's body. You don't ask your arm to reach out to pick up a pen and you don't ask your leg to take a step. You think it, and it's done. Your leg is a part of you, and the thought and the action are indistinguishable, all the intention of a single knower; and the arm or leg have no mind or will of their own. In the old man's mind Jazmin, and all the rest of humanity, were his, and had no thoughts, feelings or dreams of their own. He was all that mattered. Nothing else existed. There was no one else.

But he paid her enough to sit there, so it really didn't matter what he thought. She could study at the dining room table while he sat listening to his old records, which she'd change whenever one finished playing. The dining room table was surrounded by windows which looked out on big trees that stood next to a river. Three floors up. Pretty posh place. The sunlight from that height was dazzling, as Jazmin sat and worked on her computer or tried to read books for her courses she didn't care anything about. You don't get sunlight like that in a triple-decker on Japonica Street in Pawtucket, Rhode Island, where everything and everybody is crowded together. Even in winter, when she sat at that table, the sun warmed Jazmin's skin and the light inflamed her imagination. Sometime she dozed, warm and satisfied and on top of the world, like a lioness dozing on a hilltop after a heavy meal, warm, the top of the food chain, with no worries at all. Sometimes Jazmin just daydreamed, only half awake.

The old man was a grumpy pants, for real, but his bark was worse than his bite, and all he did was sit in that chair. Sometimes he'd call her to help him stand. His walker was next to the chair, and she'd catch his hand as he slid forward on the chair, and she'd pull as he tried to stand. She was the counter-weight that lifted him, like a drawbridge she'd once seen open over a river in the Bronx when she visited there, or the deck of a car-ferry that lifted before the ferry left the dock. He'd stand and then she'd position his walker. Then he'd totter off to the bathroom and a few minutes later he'd totter back again. Jazmin had no idea what she'd do if he fell. He weighted a hundred, maybe a hundred and ten pounds, and she thought she'd be able to lift him. But then he was so fragile, his skin thin and white, like tissue paper, his bony skull and thin arm bones visible under the skin as if he had no flesh at all. Jazmin thought he might break if you lifted him. Sometimes she thought he might break if you breathed on him too hard.

The money was good, and she could go to school, go out on weekends and still have money to give her mother at the end of the week. Fifteen bucks an hour under the table, three to eleven five days a week. Forty full hours. Sometimes they asked her to work a twelve hour shift on a weekend. Time and a half the whole day. Mr. Lewin didn't take out for lunch. There was a daughter in Boston and a son in LA. The daughter ran the show and wrote the checks.

Then the radio and Facebook started talking trash about this virus. Coronavirus. COVID-19. Whatever. Her mother thought it was a scam from Trump to scare poor people and immigrants away. Trump said it was a scam from the Democrats so they could impeach him again, or something like that. No one talks straight about anything anymore. It was hard for Jazmin to listen.

But that was all in China, so what did it matter. They had pictures of it on TV and on line, pictures of purple balls with bumps on them, like a dog toy or one of them sex things that are so nasty. Hard to imagine how those little balls could be killing people in China or would ever kill anyone here.

Then they closed the schools. Then they closed her school. Work on-line, they said. Wash your hands a lot. Stand six feet away. It didn't make no sense. Nobody Jazmin knew was sick. Just more hype, some other way to get money from poor people and immigrants, people who don't have enough money already. The old and sick, they said. You don't need to worry if you are young and healthy. At most, it will just be a cold. If it will just be a cold, what were they making so much noise about? You just can't believe anything you hear from anyone, any more.

"You'll bring me biscuits," Mr. Lewin said. It was a sunny day and late in the afternoon. There were buds that were dark red and dark green forming on the most distant branches of the trees. The spring crocuses had bloomed, and the petals of their purple and yellow flowers lay over on the ground, still bright, and the daffodils were up and just beginning to open.

"Do you have a pick-up stick?" Jazmin said.

"You'll bring biscuits. Not pretzel sticks," Mr. Lewin said.

"No, not pretzels. One of those pick-up thingees. A grabber. A contraption that lets you pick up things that are high up."

"No pick-up sticks. Biscuits."

"I need a tool that will let me hand you biscuits from far away," Jazmin said, louder than her usual voice.

"You'll bring biscuits. I'm not deaf. Biscuits, just biscuits. Not grabbers or pick-up sticks," Mr. Lewin said.

"Don't you watch the news? That virus is going around. I don't want to infect you," Jazmin said.

"You're sick?" Mr. Lewin said.

"No I'm not sick and I'm not getting sick. But they say I should stand six feet away."

"You should stay home if you're sick. Stay in bed. Drink fluids. Take Tylenol. Wash your hands every hour," Mr. Lewin said. "Don't you watch the news?"

"I'm not sick," Jazmin said.

"You'll look in the closet in the bedroom. There is a grabber there," Mr. Lewin said. "I watch the news on TV. There is a virus going around."

Jazmin didn't talk about her mother's dialysis much. It was no big deal. Three times a week. Her mother went out in the morning and came back in the afternoon all wrung out, looking brown-yellow or even a little green and shrunken like dried fruit. Just a fact of life. Kidney failure. Chronic renal failure, they called it. Her mother would end up in the hospital once or twice a year with infections or what not. But then she'd come out again. You wall it off in your mind. Jazmin's mother and brother were all she had. You live from day to day, and do what you have to do to exist, to go forward, and to protect each other. That isn't what you think about. That's just what you do.

Jazmin didn't talk about living three people in a two bedroom first floor of a triple-decker in Pawtucket either. You do what you got to do. Jazmin and her mother each had a bedroom now. Once Jazmin and her brother shared a bedroom. Now her brother slept on the couch. Crowded? Maybe a little. But it was their life and at least Jazmin's mother didn't have to climb any stairs.

First Jazmin's mother lost her sense of smell and taste. Then her nose started to run. She started to shake with chills. Then she started to cough. You don't need to be a doctor or a rocket scientist to see what it was. That virus was here now, present in Jazmin's family. It wasn't going to leave anyone out, not anyone.

Which meant Jazmin's mother was going back to the hospital. Again.

"I'm not coming in," Jazmin said on the phone.

"You're running late? How late? Speak slowly and clearly. I have a hearing impairment. You have to speak slooowly and CLEARLY when a person has a hearing impairment. Everyone knows that," Mr. Lewin said. He sounded much more alive than he did in person, as if his brain might actually still be present, someplace back in that wrinkled old head, buried beneath those beady little eyes.

"I CAN'T COME TO WORK TODAY," Jazmin said, speaking slowly and clearly.

"Don't shout," Mr. Lewin said. "I can hear you perfectly well now. You're sick?"

"I'm not sick. My mother's sick. She's in the hospital. I think she's got the virus and I don't want to spread it to you."

"You want to give the virus to your mother? Please speak slooowly and CLEARLY," Mr. Lewin said.

"MY MOTHER IS SICK. I THINK SHE HAS THE VIRUS. I DON'T WANT TO GIVE IT TO YOU," Jazmin said

"I see. Don't shout," Mr. Lewin said. "You'll come tomorrow?"

"Not tomorrow. I can't come for two weeks. If my mother is sick I have to stay home to see if I get sick," Jazmin said.

"You'll shop for me?" Mr. Lewin said. It was a strange request. Jazmin had never shopped for Mr. Lewin before.

"I can't shop for you. They said I'm supposed to say home for two weeks."

"You'll call me tomorrow?" Mr. Lewin said.

"I'll call tomorrow. If you want," Jazmin said.

"You're home alone?" Mr. Lewin said.

"I have a brother. He's sixteen."

"Your brother is sick?" Mr. Lewin said.

"No my brother is fine."

"Are you sick?"

"I'm fine. Just a precaution," Jazmin said.

"You'll call tomorrow?" Mr. Lewin said.

"I'll call tomorrow."

"What time?"

"I'll call at 10:30."

"You'll call at 9. I watch a program at 10:30."

"Okay Mr. Lewin. Anything you say. I'll call at 9."

First they put Jazmin's mother on oxygen. But they wouldn't let Jazmin or Jaime into the hospital to visit.

Jazmin and her mother FaceTimed. It drove Jazmin crazy. Not that Jazmin would have done much or said much if she had been able to visit.

They were used to the hospital. She'd just sit. Get her mother a glass of ginger ale. Get her mother toast or graham crackers from the little kitchen down the hall, the one for families. She ate some of those graham crackers dipped in milk herself, though the graham crackers often fell apart before Jazmin could eat them. Half a graham cracker would end up at the bottom of the milk carton, and would slip into her mouth, soggy and soft but surprisingly sweet, to drink instead of to eat. Jazmin's friends and her mother's friends and her brother's friends would come by the hospital. They'd have a little party in her mother's hospital room every night, and it was almost a good time. Except it wasn't. Mommie isn't going to live forever. That was the thought that Jazmin didn't ever think. Each time could be that time. She's bouncing back, this time, Jazmin thought. But she might not always.

Now Jazmin couldn't be there at all. She couldn't smell that funny hospital smell, of some chemical, some disinfectant that they tried to cover up with a fake sweet minty scent, a scent that made Jazmin's nose run. They made her mother wear a mask, in the hospital, so Jazmin couldn't see her mother's mouth when they FaceTimed. She couldn't see when the corners of her mother's mouth tilted up and twisted a little when her mother tried to suppress a smile, which was what her mother did when she was about to say something a little mean but a little true, or tease Jazmin, which was what her mother did when her mother was happy and relaxed.

FaceTime was still better than nothing. She'd see her mother's eyes and they'd talk until her mother got short of breath. Sometimes Jaime would come over and take Jazmin's phone or push his face into the frame, so he could be with Mommie too. But he was too young and a boy. Jazmin and Mommie talked. They talked about things, about people, and about what to wear, and who wore what when, not anything Jaime or any brother knew about or talked about.

And it didn't smell like Mommie over FaceTime. Her mother used a powder and had a sweet hidden smell of her own, like bath soap and talcum powder, like the pollen you smell in the springtime when the trees and flowers are in bloom.

They weren't huggy people, Jazmin and her mother, but they still touched when they were together, a hand on a hand, an arm around a shoulder. Jazmin missed that, even ached for it now. Sometimes FaceTime got Jazmin's brain confused. There was half of Mommie's face in front of her. There was Mommie sitting in a chair, talking and close, and Jazmin's brain thought Mommie was right next to her, in the room, even when she wasn't. When Jazmin looked up and saw that Mommie wasn't there, her brain shook a little and she was suddenly unsure of where she was or what, if anything, was safe and secure.

On dialysis days Jazmin's mother couldn't talk at all. They'd FaceTime for a few minutes when her mother was on the machine. But Jazmin would sign off in a hurry, so her mother's head could fall back on the pillow, so her mother could just sleep, which was all her mother had the strength for.

The phone was on ignore but it buzzed and woke her anyway. A part of Jazmin's brain never turned off. Was always awake. Was always listening. And always kept the afraid part buried.

"You're late!" the voice said. "It's eight thirty. Where are you?" It was a gravely old voice, a man's voice, lispy and slurred. No accent. English, not Spanish.

"Mr. Lewin?" Jazmin said. Her brain would have snapped *on* if the call was from the hospital or Mommie. But not now. Not for this. No way.

"You'll come *now*," Mr. Lewin said.

"It's eight-thirty in the morning," Jazmin said as she yawned. "It's not Saturday. I come in the afternoons. But I don't come anymore, remember. My mother is sick. I said I'd call at nine, not come at eight."

"You're not coming?" Mr. Lewin said.

"I told you yesterday. My mother has the virus. I don't want to bring it to you."

"Who will be here if you are not coming?" Mr. Lewin said.

"Don't you have a daughter in Boston?" Jazmin said.

"She argues, my daughter. She says I should do for myself," Mr. Lewin said.

"I get it. You want somebody there. I wish I could," Jazmin said.

"You'll come," Mr. Lewin said.

"I could Skype or FaceTime," Jazmin said.

"No. You. Now," Mr. Lewin said.

"I can't come, Mr. Lewin. I want to come. But I can't."

"I want to talk to your supervisor," Mr. Lewin said.

"I don't have a supervisor, Mr. Lewin. You know that. I'm my own boss."

"Have your supervisor call me right back," Mr. Lewin said, his voice hard as a rock, mean and cold.

Then the line went dead.

Jazmin called her mother and got no answer.

A few minutes later the phone rang again. A doctor. Her mother was intubated. They were breathing for her. She was on a machine. Stable for the moment. But really sick.

Jazmin told Jaime. They sat together in the kitchen. Jazmin got a Diet Coke. Jaime got a text and he looked down at his phone. He was there and gone, both at the same time. Then he went into the living room, where the computer was, and he went on line.

Jaime sat still for an hour. There was no place to go. No one she could to talk to. Her phone buzzed. Texts. She turned it off.

Then the door bell rang. Weird, Jazmin thought. You can't ring anyone's doorbell now. Social distancing.

"I'll get it," she yelled. Jaime had headphones on and didn't hear it anyway. *Call of Duty*, Jazmin thought, as she walked past the screen. Jaime was into it, and didn't see her at all.

There was a small white man in a dark coat with a fur collar and a black hat standing on the stoop. There was a black Lincoln Town Car with tinted windows at the curb in front of the house, its engine running, a steady stream of thin grey smoke flowing from its exhaust. The grass in front of the house had turned green since Jazmin had been outside last. There were little yellow flowers on the spindly branches of the bushes that surrounded the cement porch in front of the house.

Jazmin had mailed the rent. Her mother had it all set up. She had written rent checks a year ahead. Whenever she was in the hospital, Jazmin mailed the rent on the twenty-fifth of the month so it would be there by the first. She had mailed the check a few days before.

Jazmin wasn't wearing a mask. She put her hand over her mouth.

The landlord was an old Chinese guy, not an old white guy. The man in the hat wasn't wearing a mask either.

"You'll come," the man said.

The man in the hat was Mr. Lewin.

"I don't want to get you sick, Mr. Lewin," Jazmin said. "It's only been five days. My mother has the virus, remember? I could have the virus too."

"You'll come anyway," Mr. Lewin said.

"Mr. Lewin. I have a brother who is sixteen. He's too young to be left alone. He could have the virus too. The virus won't hurt us. But it could make you really sick. You know that?"

"I have a car and a driver. No one lives forever. You'll tell your mother."

"I can't tell my mother," Jazmin said.

Suddenly Jazmin's throat closed and she couldn't see. She was short of breath and weeping. Her knees buckled and she fell forward.

Somehow Mr. Lewin caught her. They swayed. Then Jazmin found her footing. They didn't fall.

"I could have knocked you over," Jazmin said.

"You could have come when I said come," Mr. Lewin said.

"I could make you sick, Mr. Lewin," Jazmin said.

"I have to die of something," Mr. Lewin said. "I just don't want to die alone."

"I guess we hold each other up," Jazmin said.

And then her cell phone rang. She had a siren ring tone. It was really cool. You could hear it whenever it rang. It didn't matter where you were in the house.

Mr. Lewin got sick five days later, just after Mommie's funeral. They held Mommie's body for three days to let the virus burn itself out. They don't let you have a real funeral now. Only five people. Mommie was being cremated anyway. So they had a Zoom service in Mommie's church and something like 300 people logged on. Jazmin sat in the living room next to Jaime. They each sat at their own screens so they both could see everyone. Jazmin kept the video on even though she was weeping. One part of her didn't want anyone to see. One part didn't care.

He is one tough old man, that Mr. Lewin. He got a fever and coughed and coughed and coughed. Jazmin went to his house every day to sit with him. Sometimes Jaime came, because Jazmin didn't want him to be alone. But Jaime just sat on his laptop, still dazed. *Crossfire. League of Legends. Fortnite.*

Jazmin tried and failed to study.

When Mr. Lewin stopped asking for Oreos and his English biscuits, Jazmin called 911. The EMTs came in all decked out in yellow space suits, face visors and masks, like they were attempting a moon landing. But Mr. Lewin told them to go away.

Mr. Lewin got better. It took a week, but he started to eat again. The fever disappeared. Then the cough faded, and after another week he was back to himself, back to "You'll bring me" and "Speak slooooowly and CLEARLY".

The world isn't even close to fair.

Now the lilacs are blooming. Anyway.

The Dream House

Shirley Menard was taking a wash out of the washer when she heard they hit Powerball. The phone rang but Shirley's hands were wet so she couldn't answer right then. The phone was only a few steps away but by the time Shirley dried her hands and answered the caller was gone.

"Impatient ass," she said, and she lit a cigarette.

The morning sun brought brilliant light into the shabby yellow kitchen. She opened a window. The daffodils were in bloom next to the old wooden fence behind the house, just beyond the swing set, but the kitchen still smelled like frying oil and stale cigarettes.

It was Thursday. Her only morning off. 8 A.M. and the first load was already in the dryer. She deserved a smoke.

The phone rang again.

"Powerball," a voice said.

It was Steven.

"What?" Shirley said. She had heard the "ball" but wasn't sure about the "power."

"Powerball. We won Powerball."

"*Who* won Powerball?"

"*We* won Powerball. Ernie and me. You and me. Me and Ernie split it two ways."

"How *much* Powerball? Fifty? A hundred? Two-fifty?"

"Turn on the news. The *whole* fuckin Powerball. Two hundred and fifty-eight million dollars. Two hundred and fifty-eight mill. Split two ways. We just won one hundred and twenty-nine million. Put my truck on Craigslist. I'm coming home."

"April Fools?" Shirley said.

"No April Fools. It's April, but no foolin. Turn on the TV."

Steve quit his job. Then he bought himself a powder-blue Jaguar convertible, and started driving to Newport every day to play Jai Alai.

Steven was Shirley's number three, the best of a pretty sorry bunch. Not bad looking for fifty-two. Good around Shirley's kids and grandkids. Sometimes, maybe once or twice a year, Steven brought her breakfast in bed after he had been out drinking and hadn't come to bed by the time Shirley had to get up for work. Every so often, while Shirley was washing the dishes, he'd come up behind her, put his arms around her waist, rub his chest against her back, nuzzle her neck, put his tongue in her ear, and feel her up until she turned and made out with him. In those moments Shirley though she might actually love him some.

Steven came by the nursing home two weeks after he bought the Jag, on the first warm day of spring, just as Shirley was getting off shift. He parked next to Shirley's old Honda and waited until she came out. He was wearing a new black leather driving cap, a gray leather driving jacket, and a silk blue and gold scarf. The way he looked made her laugh a little. Steven. The same man. Just not the Steven Shirley knew.

"I am taking you for a ride," he said.

"I got work to do!" Shirley said. "At home!"

"A ride," Steven said.

They drove to Newport, top down. The breeze blew through Shirley's hair. Shirley barely remembered any other life, or all the crap she had lived through.

Steven drove through Newport to Castle Hill. They sat on lawn chairs outside, smoking, each with a whiskey -- and watched sailboats come in and out of the harbor. When it started to get cold they went in, sat at the bar in a bay window, and watched the sun set. Steven had three more whiskies, got himself more than a little drunk, and talked about doing incredible things. A trip around the world. A penthouse apartment in Manhattan. A ski trip to Vail. All this money has gone to your head, Shirley said. We have a good life here. Everyone we know is here. A new house. All I want is a new house, a place by the beach, a place where I can see the ocean and hear the waves at night.

Shirley drove the Jaguar home, top down, and man could that car move, fast and incredibly smooth, more like flying than driving. The new car smell was rich and moist, even with the top down -- like honey in your coffee instead of NutraSweet, leather and wood, not the plastic and leaking-oil smell of her Honda.

Steven rattled on for a few minutes and then he fell asleep. Shirley felt weightless. She drove a little faster, just to see what the Jag could do. She remembered the dreams she had in childhood, dreams in which she floated above the telephone wires and glided from place to place, weightless, riding the air. *I don't want to change one thing*, she thought. *There is no better life. We come from the world but we live in memories and in dreams.*

The tree frogs were out when they got home to the house in Buttonwoods, singing and chirping in waves.

Shirley kept her job. She worked every day except Thursday and Saturday, first shift. It took eight years to get first shift. You don't give that up. The old people were used to her. The home had faint yellow cement block walls and smelled of disinfectant and toast.

But every day at three, the moment her shift was over, Shirley thought only about her dream house. Let Steven have his Jag. Let him buy a leather coat and a silk scarf. Let him get $40 haircuts and fancy after-shave. Let him get himself a personal trainer. Shirley wanted only one thing. A house with a water view with a private beach, like the houses investment bankers and movie stars have in magazines.

She looked at house after house, at mansion after mansion, but nothing she saw satisfied her. Agents showed her huge houses with big dining rooms and circular driveways, but Shirley wanted something different. Not more. Just different. Quietly elegant, not overwhelming, but solid as a rock and with a beautiful view. Shirley wanted a place on a hill, a place that let you see the sun rising over the ocean, where you could hear every wave break, and where you could see the sea birds flying along the coast at dawn and at dusk.

So she decided to build. First she had to find land, to find the perfect setting. She walked all over Wakefield, Saunderstown, and Matunuck in black rubber boots for three months. Finally, she found the most beautiful place on earth. It was an old dairy farm off Matunuck School House Road. The farm once raised vegetables and poultry for the rich people in Narragansett and Watch Hill, and once upon a time sent milk to the Co-Op in Wakefield, before the Co-Op closed down. The house was a mess, just a rotting brown farmhouse surrounded by maple trees set back from the road, with an overgrown walk-way made of purple flagstones, overgrown lilacs on both sides of the door, and a small red barn behind the house that had a sagging roof-line and flaking paint.

She didn't care about the farmhouse. It could be a guest house for her kids and Steven's kids when they came to stay for a week. It could just sit empty, for all she cared. The farmhouse didn't matter. What mattered to Shirley was the hill and the view of the ocean the hill provided.

To get to the hill you had to walk through two fields that been rented out to grow potatoes, and climb over two stone walls. The climb up the hill was rough going -- the woods were thick with brambles and gnarled branches of the wind-twisted trees that spread out at waist and chest level. But you could hear the waves crash and sigh as you climbed, before you could see the water. And from the top you could see a blue salt water pond half covered by lime green seagrass that waved with any breeze; you could see the beach, and beyond that you could see Block Island. Standing on that hill you could see fishing boats plying the waters of Block Island Sound; you could see freighters and cargo ships leaving Narragansett Bay for South Carolina, Europe and Africa; and sometimes you could make out the whales breaching as they swam with their calves from their winter feeding grounds in the Caribbean to their summer haunts in Buzzards Bay and north to the Bay of Fundy and to Greenland, where they fattened themselves on plankton, krill, and sea grasses.

Shirley bought the land for cash the day she saw it, right on the spot.

She hired an architect and told him to spare no expense. The house needed to face the sea.

Shirley had just gotten by for long enough. Now she wanted a house that was solid and tight, a house that would stand against the wind, a house that let her feel the sea and hear the sea at night from the bedrooms on the second floor, a house in which she could feel the sea and hear the sea from the kitchen during the day while she was cooking, when the kids came for dinner and their kids chased one another from room to room. She didn't want the floor to shake when some kid ran down the hall. She wanted to hear the wind blow around the house, but she didn't want to hear the wind to rattle the windows anymore and she didn't want to feel a draft or a chill when the wind blew in mid-winter ever again. You needed to smell the sea, and hear the sea, but the house had to be solid and tight so you could sleep soundly, without worrying, even when a nor'easter hit or when a hurricane came up the coast in September.

After the architects came the contractor. Contractors. She fired a couple along the way. Contractors are like husbands. They tell you what they think you want to hear, until they get what they want. Then they fall asleep. Only the last contractor was any good, and that was only because Shirley was always there. He did whatever Shirley told him to do.

She came every day after work. Forty-five minutes down, forty-five minutes back. Traffic made the trip longer in the summer when the whole world went to South County at five o'clock. Shirley talked to all the subs, and she checked, every day, to make sure she was getting what she paid for. She had hopes. And dreams. And expectations.

They were going to have a perfect house. Simple as that. Simply perfect.

Steven drove his powder-blue Jaguar to Newport and to Twin Rivers during the day. He came down to Matunuck once when she found the farm, and another time after they cleared the land on the top of the hill. But he didn't love the construction. The contractor bulldozed a long dirt drive out of the hillside which was brown mud when it rained and brown dirt when it was dry. Steven said he didn't want to get the Jaguar all messed up, so he didn't come again. He started getting his hair dyed black, and going to the gym.

At last the house was done, and Shirley was able to get the long driveway paved. They laid down a layer of asphalt, so the surface of the road was smooth and flat as it snaked up the hillside. Then Shirley had them lay on a few inches of crushed gray-blue stone, and had that steam-rolled into the asphalt, so the surface looked like it was gravel, but it wasn't. Nothing loose. Nothing that would kick up dirt or mud. A ribbon through the countryside, climbing a low hill between a farm and the sea. Like the long circular drive leading up to a country mansion, which this was, for them. Their country mansion. Their dream house. It wasn't really very big. Nothing too showy. Picture perfect. Solid, classic, secure. Mansion enough for Shirley.

And then she got them ready to move. Cleaned out the garage, attic and basement. Threw out stuff she had accumulated for 30 years. Bought new furniture. Saved a couple of pieces – a divan from her grandmother, a sideboard from her mother, and a rocking chair from her first house and first husband, the one she nursed both her kids in. But sent the rest of the junk to Goodwill. Called the movers. Picked a date.

Steven called at ten-thirty from Foxwoods, boozed up but still sweet.

"I'm comin' home," he said, slurring his words. "Moving tomorrow. Comin' home now."

"Stay there. Get a room. Sober up, and come home in the morning. The movers get here at nine," Shirley said. *Here we go again,* she thought. *I've been down this road before. Same shit, different day. Déjà vu all over again.*

"You need me. Home. Tonight. Promised," Steven said. Drunk as he was, he heard that Shirley was pissed.

"I need you alive."

"Come get me?"

"Just sleep there tonight," Shirley said. She needed this like a hole in the head. He wasn't alone and she knew it. She had been down this road before. It didn't matter. If she had to move into the house alone, so be it. At least she'd have the sea. "I got plenty to do. Go get some sleep, and just get yourself up in time, so you are here at nine."

"Need to get home."

"Go to sleep. You're no good to me drunk, and it wouldn't look good if you crashed the Jag the night before we moved in. Get a room, and get here first thing in the morning ready to work."

"G'night. Need to be there."

"Get a some sleep. I'll see you tomorrow. Now good night."

Shirley didn't sleep. She had a house. But here she was, sleeping alone.

That night the house filled her dreams which turned into nightmares. The Jag came through her window only there was a shark where its front end was supposed to be, and the shark had its mouth wide open, its teeth made of metal and its headlights black and rolled back into its head. The Matunuck house was hovering in the air, and all the parts that Shirley had chosen -- the cherry banister, the granite countertop, the stainless steel refrigerator, the stone vanity -- all the pieces were falling one by one through the floor and plunging into the sea. Artie, her wimpy first husband, now twice the size he'd ever been and covered with tattoos, was standing over her, a big kitchen knife where his penis was supposed to be.

Then it was morning. Birds back from winter began to call and sing in the boxwoods by the back fence, next to the swing-set. There was misty blue and gray light in the window. Then trees, telephone poles, houses and cars folded out of the blue mist.

Shirley fell back to sleep. It was a deep sleep, and she didn't dream.

The blurting beep of a truck's backup alarm woke her. Car doors slammed. There was a knock on the door before Shirley could push the covers back and throw on a robe.

It was Steven. He was here after all. Sobered up, sweet and sorry and ready to move.

A dream come true. They were moving together to the dream house. Shirley had worried for nothing.

Why had she worried? Why had she doubted him?

We come from the world but we live in our memories and our dreams.

Winning Couple Perish in Fiery Crash. (Turn to Ten News) Just two weeks after claiming a half share in a Powerball winning ticket, a Warwick couple perished in a fiery crash on Route Four, just south of Wickford. The driver of the car, traveling at speeds estimated by police to be over 110 miles an hour, appears to have lost control of the vehicle at the Route 102 overpass. The vehicle left the roadway and flipped over before exploding. Both occupants of the vehicle were killed instantly. Identification of the driver and passenger is pending notification of next of kin.

The Failure of Family Medicine

3/17/2016

<u>Progress Note</u>:

<u>New to Establish.</u>

<u>Chief Complaint</u>: "tired and hunger pains x 3 days."

<u>History of Present Illness</u>: 36-year-old English speaking Hispanic female with fatigue and abdominal pain of three days duration. The fatigue is so severe that the patient wasn't able to get out of bed two days in a row – very unusual for her – and her two girls, ages five and seven, had to wake her in the morning so they could get to school on time. Usually it's the other way around. The patient works in an office as a receptionist and never misses work but she did have to work an eleven-hour day on Monday which was okay for her – she likes the overtime and her girls go to her mother in Pawtucket after work. The abdominal pain actually started last June and keeps her up at night. It's burning and boring, comes and goes, but when it comes on it's there for weeks at a time and is associated with burping and belching. It is worse when she lays down, better when she stands or walks, the same feeling she gets when she is hungry only ten times worse. No nausea, vomiting, or diarrhea. No blood in the stool or black tarry stools. No fever or chills. Not emotionally stressed. She lives with her girls who she says are her whole world. Sleeps ok except for the discomfort. Poor appetite. No medications. Doesn't smoke. Drinks occasionally. Needs a note for work – reports that her boss is a good person but very precise and says she needs a doctor's note if she's out more than a day or two, but she likes her boss who she says is fair but strict. She was seen at an urgent care center two weeks prior for the same abdominal pain but without the fatigue when the pain was keeping her up at night

and the clinic wasn't open. They ordered an ultrasound which she is going to have tomorrow. Her boss knows about that already and understands she will be in late so the out of work note she needs is only for yesterday and today.

Review of Systems: No trouble swallowing. No cough or wheezing. No chest pain or pressure. Exercises regularly. Regular periods but very heavy flow. No back pain or muscle pain. Nerves and emotions ok. Mood good, but worries about her girls from time to time. Doesn't see or hear things that might not be there. No thoughts of hurting herself or anyone else. Had diabetes with her pregnancies that resolved after her children were born.

Physical Examination: Is remarkable only for epigastric tenderness. No masses, spasm or rebound. No Murphy's sign. Normal bowel sounds.

Laboratory Studies: Blood sugar 146 (elevated but she just ate). Hemoglobin A1c 6.1.

Assessment and Plan:
   #1. Fatigue and hunger pains. Likely recurrent diabetes. Will refer to nutrition for diabetic diet and teaching. Start metformin 500 mg twice a day. Consider and test for Lyme disease (fatigue), anemia from blood loss (heavy periods), gall bladder inflammation (fat, forty, and fecund).

   #2. Abdominal pain. Possible gall bladder. For sonogram elsewhere. Will ask patient to have the radiologist send us the results.

Recheck 3 months.

When I met Julio it felt like the world had flipped over, turned itself inside out and righted itself again. After I threw the girls' father out, that two timing son of a bitch, I thought I was done with men and that my girls would be enough for me forever. Sure I went out on Friday nights. You have to get dressed up, put a little makeup on, drink a little and dance a little once in a while otherwise you don't feel like you are alive. My mother would come over to be with the girls. Mostly it was girl talk and girls dancing with each other. The men would come sniffing around, pretty ghetto, lots of bling and baseball hats, thinking themselves so hot but there was nothing there, no one to take seriously.

But Julio, now there was a different kind of man -- serious, smart and adult, dark and quiet and really good looking like one of those men in the newspaper who model men's suits. We met at the wedding of my boss's daughter, who was marrying a guy from Boston. Very smart people. Smart and successful. I didn't think there were going to be any Spanish people at the wedding, which was at a very pretty place in Bristol overlooking the ocean. Me and the other girls from the office, we were on our best behavior, and I was thinking, pretty night, pretty bride, the girls and I would sit together and talk and then we'd dance like we do at the office Christmas party when only the girls dance and the men, they just sit there and drink beer.

You sometimes don't really see the person who sits next to you at a table because you have to turn to look and that's not polite if you don't know the person. I was talking to the girls when Julio came to the table. He was alone but he went around the table, from person to person, introducing himself and saying, "Julio Mendez, party of the groom. Julio Mendez, party of the groom. Julio Mendez, party of the groom." Very formal and polite, like he was the principal of a school or the captain of a ship. Dark suit, dark thinning hair, dark smart eyes that kept to themselves, but he looked at you, just for a moment, and his eyes didn't go right from your face to your chest, the way half the men in the world behave. Big shoulders but not tall, maybe a little taller than me but not much and a strong grip when he shook your hand, strong and warm like he was learning you with his grip and really wanted to know what made you tick from the way you squeezed his hand.

He was wearing a pink almost purple silk tie that stood out, that was different from how the rest of him looked. That said, there is something different about this man, something alive inside – some kind of courage or pride or passion, that said how he looks and acts might not be all of who he is. Anyway he sits down next to me and I don't look at him and he sits there, quiet for a few minutes. He knows I'm Spanish and I know he's Spanish but neither of us are saying anything and I'm waiting for him to turn to me or for me to turn to him and for one of us to make a little joke in Spanish about being Spanish at a place where there weren't any others, about waiters or something, the kind of thing Spanish people say to ourselves about each other when no one else is looking but he doesn't do that at all. He turns to me and says, "I'd like to know you better. Tell me about your life," which is not what you expect to hear from a man you are sitting next to at a table at a wedding and he says it in English, this beautiful clear formal English he speaks as if he's Castilian and is speaking English Castilian and I talk to him in English.

I tell him about my life and my girls. He's listening, asking questions, and he really gets me, like he knows something about what I had to live through with the girls' father, like there are things he's had to live through himself but he doesn't talk about those things. I'm liking the strength in this man who has feelings and a good brain, who has a heart but doesn't wear his heart on his sleeve. That's what strength is. We talk English to each other always. Except later, when we talk Spanish to each other in bed.

5/1/2016

Progress Note

Same day acute. 36-year-old Hispanic female with abdominal pain and trouble sleeping. Still uncomfortable and did not want to wait for scheduled follow-up. Lots of burning in the chest which keeps her up at night. The chest pain is midline, not on the left. Does not travel to the left arm or shoulder. Worse when she lies down. Not worse with walking or climbing stairs – and walks four to six blocks a day to the bus which she uses to travel to work but no regular exercise program. Not short of breath with walking. Work is busy but not stressful. Does not eat a low cholesterol or limited calorie diet. Drinks two to three cups of coffee a day and a glass of wine or two each night to relax after her children are in bed. Not a smoker. Pain is still like a hunger pain. Did not take the metformin.

Physical Examination: Reveals no chest tenderness, no pleural or pericardial rub, normal heart sounds with no murmur, good breath sounds equal on both sides. Abdomen soft not tender without rebound or spasm and normal bowel sounds. Extremities without swelling or edema. Patient appears anxious.

Laboratory Studies: Lyme Titers negative. Hemoglobin 12. Low normal. Normal Hemoglobin A1c 6.0 today. Ultrasound elsewhere reported by patient to be normal.

Assessment and Plan:

> #1. Chest pain. Rule out heart disease. Check cholesterol and stress echo. Might consider reflux gastritis if normal.

> #2. Diabetes controlled by diet and exercise. Ok to wait on metformin. Reinforced nutrition consult which is booked for two months hence – diabetes teaching has a big backlog.

Return to clinic one month, after stress test done. To call for more chest pain. To call 911 and go to the Emergency Room for chest pain that lasts more than three minutes, that feels like someone is standing on your chest or that you feel in the left arm or shoulder.

I thought Julio would call me but he didn't call me and for a while I forget about him. You know how it is. You meet someone and I don't know, they make you pay attention in a different sort of way and you think, maybe, cool, maybe more, and then they don't call you and the girls need this and that and then you forget about that person you met.

So, a few weeks later I see my cousin Yvette at La Casona and she says, "I heard you met my husband's brother Julio and that he thought you were very hot," and I say, "Who?" and then I remember and I guess I start to turn colors or something so she pushes me a little, kind of like a love tap, and she says, "Oh, oh I see the way it is," and I say, "It's not nothing. I met the guy and never hear another word from him so what good is that," and she says, "He's a very good man and he's been through a lot" and then she gives me the lowdown: he has a wife and three kids but the wife is more than a little crazy, in and out of the loony-bin, so he takes care of the kids who are now teenagers and he takes care of the wife when she is good enough to be home but that he is mostly alone. So he doesn't call me because he can't call me.

And then it's the summer and Yvette calls up and says bring the girls to the Colombian Festival which is Sunday so I bring the girls and my mother and we are standing in the middle of that field looking at the exhibits and so forth and listening to a band that is playing Colombian music but way too loud and then it starts to rain. The girls are running around somewhere so I find them and go to the big T-Mobile tent to get out of the rain and I'm standing there with the girls and a man comes in, he's holding a program book over his head to keep the rain off and it's Julio. "Hey," I say. "Hey," he says. And then I introduce the girls and my mother.

6/1/2016

Progress Note

Follow-up. 36-year-old Hispanic female with abdominal pain and trouble sleeping. Much more burping and belching. Pain still present, worse at night. Radiates to left shoulder. Not present with walking or climbing stairs. Nausea, no vomiting. Anxious but no feelings of impending dread when the pain is present. Pain lasts for hours. No shortness of breath. Everything at home and work ok. Stress echo pending, was rescheduled by patient. Hemoglobin A1c 5.8 today. No diabetic teaching yet. Did not start metformin. Watching calories and walking everyday (to the bus).

Physical Examination: Clear lungs. Heart regular rate and rhythm. Abdomen soft not tender. No Murphy's sign. ?epigastric tenderness. Extremities without edema.

Assessment and Plan:

> #1. Rule out heart disease. Needs to be careful with exertion until stress echo done - is walking to the bus every day -- but is to call 911 for crushing chest pain.

> #2. Diabetes. Controlled by diet and exercise. Watching calories and exercising.

Soon Julio starts to come around. He's shy about it. Very proper. "I have a question about my kids," he says. "Could I buy you lunch and pick your brain," he says on the phone.

"I only get half hour for lunch," I say.

"Okay how about dinner?"

We meet.

"The girls are with my mother-in-law after school and she spoils them," he says. "I make them wash the dishes and do their homework. They are thrilled to stay with their grandmother – she lets them watch TV and eat junk food all the time."

His kids are 18, 17, and 15. He doesn't want them sitting on the computer all night or watching TV but that's all they do, watch TV on the computer in their rooms. They need the computer for homework. Is he wrong? Or just old fashioned?

"No," I say. "They need to sleep and they need to read. Make a rule. No computer after nine PM. And then turn the router off every night at nine."

"They'll watch on their smart-phones," he says.

"Take their smart-phones every night at nine," I say. "Give the phones back at breakfast. That way they'll eat breakfast."

"They need to talk to their friends," he says.

"It's after nine. They need to sleep," I say."

"But they say it's not cool," he says.

"You have a landline?" I say. "If they need to talk, let them use the landline. You can watch that."

"They say that is so awkward," he says. "They say that makes them different."

"You are the father," I say. "You love them and want them to succeed. They need to be different. There is plenty of time for them to be cool when they are twenty-two and on their own. Enough kids go ghetto already."

"You are so smart," he says. "Way smarter than me."

He never says a word about the mother of these kids. He drops me at my house, thanks me, and shakes my hand, like we are in a business meeting or something.

Then he calls the next week.

Every week he needs advice. About his mother, who is living in Baltimore. About his business. He owns a little company that makes electrical things, circuit boards and switches, that he started fifteen years ago in his basement because he has a good head for math and a good head for engineering which is what he went to college for in Colombia. He has twenty-seven employees who always fight with each other, and endless drama. All of a sudden I am an expert at kids, at families, at labor relations, and all of a sudden he needs my advice about all these things.

Some weeks I don't hear from him. I'm guessing then his wife is home or acting up. Julio never complains.

But one night at dinner I say, "tell me how your wife is this week," and his eyes get dark and he starts with a whisper.

"She's stable," he says. "She's home and everything is under control."

That night his handshake turns into an embrace. I kiss him on the cheek and he holds me to him, hard and close, as if he is holding on for dear life.

7/12/2016
Progress Note
Did not keep appointment.

We go to Slater Park on Sundays. We do the Carousel, which the girls love, but mostly we sit in the park and the girls run free. They do the playground and they run down to the lake pretending to be this and that, and sometimes they meet other kids in the playground and they create a whole little telenovela that unfolds on the banks of the lake and has them running in and out of the trees and hiding behind the kiosks and the out-buildings, while Julio and I sit in the sunlight and talk.

He is an attentive man, that Julio, but tense. One day as we get ready to leave I see him stop and fall back and then try to stand again and then stop again, his face set and serious, and then he struggles slowly to his knees and from his knees to his feet.

"What is it?" I say.

"It's nothing," he says. "Just my back. A little pain. A little spasm."

"I can fix the back," I say, laughing, because it is beautiful out and he is a beautiful man and I feel like I can fix anything and everything and that life it is so good. And when he stands I come behind him and put my hands on his shoulders and start to give him just a small massage. The muscles in his shoulders and neck are big and stronger than I ever imagined and they are tight like the steel cables that hold bridges up. His tight back muscles do not loosen much when I try to knead them as if they were dough but Julio says, "Bueno," which is the first Spanish word he ever says to me, and then he turns quickly away from me, as if I have hurt him.

Suddenly his face is very dark.

"It is good," I say. "It is okay. Come to my house after 9:30 when the girls are in bed. It is okay Julio."

"I cannot go to your house," he says. "It is not proper."

"It is okay," I say.

And he turns and walks stiffly away. I can see the pain in his back, how he feels a jolt with each step in his back and neck which are locked in spasm, like a cable being wound by a winch.

That night he comes to my house after 9:30 after the girls are in bed and he stays only until midnight.

Later I learn that he is parking his car around the corner and down the block so no one can tell.

After that he comes to my house many nights between 9:30 and midnight, and I give him a key, and sometimes he comes between 4 am and 6 am so he's gone when the girls get up, and nobody knows and everybody knows at once, and I am loving him and I am not ashamed.

9/20/2016

Progress Note

Open Access/ Same Day Acute. 36-year-old Hispanic female with abdominal pain and trouble sleeping. DNKA last visit because she was feeling better. Now pain and trouble sleeping again. Had stress-echo which was normal. Still has chest pain and abdominal pain suddenly worse at night, keeping her from sleeping. Sleeping less - only a few hours a night now. Not exercising. Drives to work. No new stresses. Family status unchanged. Single mother of two young daughters. Doesn't smoke or drink. Not concerned about her personal safety because of any relationship issues - no intrapartner violence. No change in diet - eats fruits and vegetables - some but not too much citrus or other acidy foods. Has been drinking milk and taking Tums at night and that helps her to sleep.

Physical Examination: Mucus membranes pink. Clear lungs. Cardiac regular rate and rhythm. Abdomen soft with moderate epigastric tenderness - replicates pain! No mass or other tenderness. No rebound. Extremities not tender without edema.

Assessment and Plan:
> #1.Reflux gastritis, rule out H. Pylori. Check H. Pylori titers. Start Prilosec 20mg daily for 30 days. Recheck one month.

And then Julio's wife improves. Suddenly she is awake and alert and making dinner. Cleaning the house. Paying the bills like she used to do, once upon a time. Asking about his day.

Maybe it is the medicine. Maybe her brain was injured and has healed. Maybe it is an act of God. I wonder if it isn't me, if they aren't bad for each other, and when Julio is with me his wife has the space she needs to live. Maybe she knows about me, and makes herself recover to get him back, as if her illness was just the way she talked to him, the way for her to get his attention away from his kids and his work. It doesn't matter. She is better. She is awake and alert and she knows that something is going on. That I am going on.

I know that Julio never thought this was possible. That he came to me in sadness and loneliness, mourning his wife, his family and his marriage, but now he is torn in two. I know he loves me and that he respects his wife but he doesn't love her. I know that he now likes his wife again but he doesn't love her. I know he loves me, that he loves my girls and everything that is false about the world becomes true for him when he talks to me, when I lie in his arms.

I stop sleeping. He comes now once a week and doesn't stay long. He looks dark, the way he looked when we met.

I am glad for him. I am glad for his wife. My girls are sad. They think about him, and they are sad. They think about me, and they are sad. His children brighten, and do better in school.

I am not sleeping. There is an ache in my chest where my heart should be. An ache, not a pain. There is a burning. I am sitting up all night. A part of me is always listening for his key in the door. He is a good man, an honest man, a man of principle and tremendous integrity.

It was not like this with the father of the girls. The father of the girls, he just used me, flattered me, and tricked me. I was nothing to him and when the time came I threw him out because I always knew he was no good. This is different. I love Julio.

So I end it.

Then it feels like I will never sleep again.

10/20/2016

Progress Note

Follow-up. H. Pylori gastritis. 36-year-old Hispanic female with abdominal pain and trouble sleeping. Some improvement with Prilosec but still not sleeping. Burping and gas much less. Burning and chest pain less. Some nausea, no vomiting or diarrhea. No appetite. Not bloated. Hunger pain gone but still left with an empty feeling. Mood down. Sad but not hopeless. Not sexually active. No suicidal or homicidal ideation. Doesn't like the short days or the winter.

Physical Examination: Lungs clear. Heart regular rate and rhythm. Abdomen soft, not tender, normal bowel sounds no mass. Extremities without edema.

Laboratory: H. pylori was positive

Assessment/Plan:

> #1. H. Pylori Gastritis. Add Lansoprazole 30mg twice daily for 14 days. Amoxicillin 500mg twice daily for 14 days and Clarithromycin 500mg twice daily for 2 weeks. Possible side effects – diarrhea and a metallic taste in the mouth. The importance of taking all the medicine reviewed in detail.

> #2. Depression versus Seasonal Affective Disorder. Trial of bright light 30 minutes twice daily for one month. Recheck then. If no improvement, consider behavioral health referral.

Recheck 4 to 6 weeks.

At 4:30 in the morning I think I hear a key in the lock. I have not forgotten Julio but I have put him out of my mind. Ancient history. Sadness. Don't go there. You live and you learn. But now I am thinking about the girls' father who I haven't seen or heard from in two years but who still has a key and it is like him to come sneaking around when he's in trouble or when his girl of the moment has thrown him out. Sneaking around or worse. He has done me worse. I thought once to buy a gun so I would be ready for him when he comes around again but I don't have the stomach for that and I don't want it in the house for the girls to see or the girls to find. But I do have a baseball bat. A metal bat from softball. Once when I was a girl I played.

The noise goes away.

I open the door. There are flowers between the front door and the storm door. From Julio. It's four-thirty in the morning. I am looking for him but all I see are the red tail lights of a car driving away. Julio is gone. He was here. And he is gone again.

12/1/2016
Progress Note
Follow-up. 36-year-old Hispanic female with abdominal pain and trouble sleeping. Abdominal pain resolved. No burping. No belching. No bloating. Mood improved. Not sleeping well though. Often wakes at 4 A.M. but then able to go back to sleep so often gets 7 hours a sleep a night in total. Using a light with daylight spectrum an hour or two a day as instructed. Appetite fair. Not stressed. No suicidal or homicidal ideation. Not seeing or hearing things that aren't there. No chest pain.

Physical Examination: Lungs clear. Heart regular rate and rhythm. Abdomen soft without masses. No Murphy's sign or rebound. Extremities without swelling or edema.

Assessment and Plan:
> #1. Reflux gastritis. Resolved.
>
> #2. Seasonal Affective Disorder. Effectively treated with light therapy.
>
> #3. Sleep Disorder – early awakening. Sleep hygiene reviewed. On awakening patient is to get out of bed and read for at least twenty minutes or until she feels sleepy and then return to bed. No TV in bed. Use bed only for sleep or sex.

Return to clinic in 3 to 4 months for regular health maintenance examination. Will recheck hemoglobin then and consider iron for heavy periods.

One day I call him up at his place during the day.

"Stop bringing flowers," I say. "I love the flowers but it isn't flowers I want. I can't sleep Julio. I want you back but all of you not just flowers in the middle of the night."

"I am sorry," he says. "I thought you would be pleased. I still think about you. All the time."

"Thinking about me doesn't do anybody any good," I say. "It's very nice that you like me. It's even very nice that you love me. But loving and liking aren't the same thing as two people being together. I need someone for me, or no one. And I need someone for my girls."

Then I don't hear from him for two weeks.

"I gave my word," he says, when he calls me. "This is not your problem it is my problem. I promised I would take care of her in sickness and in health. She is better now and that is good. But what is inside me isn't better."

"I don't care anymore what is inside you," I say. "You are ripping me to pieces. Love me or let me alone."

He knocks on the door one night after the girls are in bed. He is looking dark like he is angry at me.

"I'm going to stay married to her," he says.

"Why are you here?" I say. "You are making it worse for me, not better."

"I am going to stay married to her but I want to live here with you."

"Nice," I say, "very nice. You get your cake and eat it. What about my girls? Don't you think they need a real father? And what about your kids? They need a father too."

"I thought you'd be happy to see me," he said. "Maybe I shouldn't have come."

"Shit or get off the pot," I say. "I do love you but you are tearing me apart."

"What I came to say is that I am going to stay married to her but we will make this work. I found a clean three family on Transit Street. A beautiful old house. Four bedrooms in the upstairs apartment. Three bedrooms in the downstairs. It has a big yard and a carriage house."

"And you want us all to live together? Are you crazy? You want me to live in a triple-decker?" I say. "How very convenient. What about your wife?"

"It's not a triple-decker," he says. "It's a real house. My wife knows all about you," he says. "You were her shock therapy. She got better. But we didn't. She and I didn't get better. She knows it is you and me now. And it sucks, but this is the best I can do. Maybe someday she finds someone else and we divorce. But not now. Now I am with the kids and I am with you and we find a way to make a family out of the terrible mess I have made."

"You didn't make a mess," I say. "You got a mess. Now you are trying to make lemonade out of lemons. But I don't know if I can do this."

"I don't expect you to," he says."

It's too crazy. I don't know what I will say to his wife, who I only feel sorry for. I don't know what I will say to his kids or how they will look at me. How they will think about me. I don't know how his wife will be able to stand it. Or me. Maybe it will make her crazy again. Or me. Or both of us together.

But then I feel like I know his kids from all he has told me about them. He is twisting himself in knots for me. For my kids. For his kids. For us. What about the third apartment? I say. It's in the carriage house. I want it for my mother, I say. That's why a three family, he says.

And then, as crazy as it is, I think I will do this thing. We will probably kill each other or him or we will fight and it will wear us out but it just could work. Suddenly I want to meet them all, his kids, even his wife, and make them feel as good about themselves as he makes me feel about living.

This is nuts but he is a good man.

So I throw him out again, this time for good.

6/1/2017
Progress Note
First Prenatal Visit. 37-year-old Hispanic Female. Last Menstrual Period 4/12/2017. Positive pregnancy test. Risk Factors: Advanced maternal age. Iron deficiency Anemia. History of Depression. Adult onset Diabetes Mellitus, diet controlled. Estimated Date of Delivery 1/16/2018.

Stand Clear of the Closing Doors Please

Roland Chesney felt outside himself when he came back to the city for the general strike. The city was in his blood, the same as it had been when he had lived there 40 years before -- but also overwhelmingly different. The grid of streets were the same as they had always been, a logical layout, in numerical order, so you always knew where you were. The avenues were logical as well, once you learned the named ones – Lexington, Park and Madison on the East Side, where he never used to go – Amsterdam and Columbus, his city, once, aka Ninth and Tenth Avenues above 59th Street - and Broadway cutting kitty-cornered from east to west as you went north, the hypotenuse, which let you walk or bike from the Upper West Side, where real people sometimes lived, to the Lower East Side, where real people always lived, back in the day. Roland knew the city -- or at least Manhattan and the Bronx -- like the back of his hand. It was tattooed into his brain, memory resident, so elemental that he didn't have to think about it, he could just look up and know where he was, and without thinking he always knew the best way to get from one place to the next.

That said, an enormous amount had changed. The double A, the Eighth Avenue local, which had always been his lifeline, his aorta, was gone. The twin towers, which he had watched go dark in the blackout of 1977 from his place on 5th Street and Second Avenue, were long gone as well, collapsed into clouds of toxic dust, falling steel and bodies flying through the air, twenty years ago. The particularly toxicity of race and class in New York was less intense than it was, less palpable on every street and in every interaction between people who looked different. The perception among white people and people of a certain social class regardless of race, that blackness meant danger and social inferiority, and the dismay, abandonment, isolation and anger that perception engendered in the hearts of people of color, who were and felt excluded, had once poisoned these streets and avenues with fear, despair and anger. It had been a perception unrelated to ideology and thus particularly painful, so that people who would say all men are created equal would cross the street when a young man of color was walking behind them; so that those people expected that every chambermaid, doorman, street sweeper, ticket taker, train station porter, cabdriver and garment district porter to be Black, and without real personhood, and so that those people rarely met the gaze of Black people in the streets. White people and the power structure they built dismissed and disregarded great swaths of the city – Harlem, the Bronx, Bed-Stuy, the Lower East Side and all housing projects – considering those places to be places that no civilized person would ever go.

The city was different now, at least to the gaze of a white man. Not completely changed, but different from what it had been. Black people were still hassled and shot down by police. But the chambermaids, the street sweepers and the garbage collectors were now Central American, Guatemalans and Hondurans. White hipsters had invaded Harlem and Bed-Stuy, and people of all colors walked everywhere in the city, without encountering the glare or the gaze of not belonging. Queens had become a United Nations, a quilt of languages and cultures, where cab drivers from all nations lived. The

Bronx had been re-created as a middle class place – mostly inhabited by people of color now, but now middle class people of color, like the Bronx Roland remembered from childhood, stable neighborhoods on Gun Hill Road, Fordham Road and University Heights, and not anything like the warzone the Bronx had been in the seventies, when it was on fire and the streets ran between collapsed buildings and fields of rubble, when the Bronx looked like Dresden after the war, as if the Germans had bombed us to submission and not the other way around. Now Third Avenue in the Bronx, where the old El used to be, was bright and sunny, and lined with banks that had drive-in tellers, fast food joints and chain stores with bright signs in red, yellow, green and blue. Now Third Avenue looked like any commercial strip in America, the same stores, the same parking lots, the same signs, in an America where every place looks like every other place, the strange, perverse equality of consumer capitalism. Now the people of color on the streets of Manhattan were often well dressed and self-confident, and people looked one another in the eye as they walked past.

The trash was gone from the streets. There were flowers in the flowerbeds in all the parks and on the Avenues. People were said to be safe in Central Park and Morningside Park. The graffiti, the brilliant, bold yellow, green and blue twisting emanations of color, the repressed soul of a tortured people, was gone from the subway cars, and the city itself, which most people had feared, was now filled with tourists and with light, although too many too tall buildings cast long shadows over the avenues, and kept the cross streets in gloom.

A general strike. It seemed unbelievable. The spirit of 1848, suddenly manifest in America. People rising up after four years of repression. The common good rising up, beating back the crass commercialism of American life. Democracy infusing freedom. Justice defeating greed. The life of the mind dominant and narcissism cowering in defeat. Who could have imagined that summer of love was still present, hibernating in the dark recesses of the American soul?

Roland had come out of his hiding place in Western Massachusetts to be there, to add his voice to three or four million other voices. It was said there would be people all the way north from 42nd street and that the crowd would fill the park up to Sheep's Meadow and beyond, past 110th street up into the Bronx, and that they would march on Wall Street together. The time had come. Bad ideas and bad faith had imprisoned a culture, had polluted the air and wrecked the climate, had made virtual slaves of three generations of young people who had deigned to educate themselves, had jailed three generations of Black men and drug poisoned three generations of poor white people, and now, finally, it was time to pay the piper, as now, finally, people were rising up. The bridges and roads would be filled with people. The clerks and porters and salesclerks and sanitation men would join with college students and high school teachers and doctors and nurses and lawyers streaming in from Brooklyn and the Bronx and Queens. There were people on all the bridges, and the ferries from Staten Island were jam packed with people who sang songs and carried signs, who flowed over the top deck and leaned over the railings. Manhattan was being occupied by the pure products of America, who were reclaiming the city at last.

Or that was the plan. He was one small man, with one small life. Yesterday he was certain that everything he had lived for was impossible, that his beliefs were meaningless, an illusion. Today it seemed as though anything and everything was possible, that what was dead inside him was coming back to life, and that his dreams, the dreams of a generation, and perhaps, of all human kind, were finally to be realized, that all those years of marching, organizing and hoping had not been in vain.

It was April and still cold, but the sun was strong. The leaves were not yet back on the trees, but the birds were back, the robins, their red-orange breasts flashes of hope in a hum colored world, hopping and flitting with the city sparrows, who had overwintered in the city and seemed to be able to survive anything. Roland had a scarf wrapped around his neck against the cold, and wore a green down jacket and hiking boots, and he walked quickly when he came out of the subway at 59th Street.

Here. They were supposed to meet here, right in front of the statute of Columbus. Where they had parted ways so long ago. In fifteen minutes.

The sun warmed his face and the huge crowd lifted him up, a sensation he hadn't felt in years, as if he had just become bigger than himself, way bigger, like the bridegroom in that fragment from Sappho, or a Greek prophet at Delphi, infused with the spirit of the gods. Columbus Circle. Once the center of his emotional life. Always the center of his city. The Coliseum used to be there. It was now gone. Around the corner from Carnegie Hall. Not so far from the Museum of Modern Art, or the corner, on 54th and Sixth Avenue, where Moon Dog, the blind prophet of a lost era, used to sit in his Viking headgear, hum his music, sell books and bric-a-brac, and bear witness to the emptiness of the corporate American soul. The Huntington Hartford Museum had been there for a while. It was gone as well, but that didn't matter, because no one Roland knew had ever been inside it. Columbus Circle was where he changed trains, where he walked to when he was going anywhere in the city, what he thought about whenever he had to think of going anywhere, as in, – how far a place was from Columbus Circle – could he walk there, which train did he need to take to get there, and whether and where he'd need to change trains. Geographers use Columbus Circle to measure the distance from any place in the world to New York. So it was the center of the world of others as well, at least to the extent that New York was the center of the world, which it might have been, for a brief, fleeting moment in history, at least in the mind of New Yorkers. Like Roland. Who would always be a New Yorker, long after he stopped living in New York.

He hadn't been in love with her, and she knew it. She was the one who had the courage to walk away. He had been lying to himself. She knew what he pretended not to know, and she acted while he was only drifting, taking the easy way out. Comrades, yes. Lovers, for a time. But not in love. That was the challenge, wasn't it? Being able to love first. And then loving, in fact.

It would be twenty years before he unlocked that puzzle, and by then it was too late.

The bands were lined up and brigades were forming on Eighth Avenue above the park, like they did before the Macy's Thanksgiving parade, only today they wouldn't stop at the Museum of Natural History, the way they did on Thanksgiving with their silly balloons. Today there would be high school bands and choruses from all over, a line that stretched up through Harlem and over High Bridge into the Bronx, the Pronk folks mixed in with cheerleaders from the high schools, and life sized puppets from Bread and Circus and Big Nazo scattered in among the VFW, the mummers and the ladies from the Order of the Eastern Star. More than amazing. A people standing up together to defend themselves and their democracy. Who would have thought it? Roland thought of all the little meetings and little demos he had attended over the years. Five people in a library. Seven people in a storefront. Three people in a living room. Stupid little demos to try to prevent the invasion of Iraq, or to stand in solidarity with the people of Hong Kong, or Syria, or Nicaragua or Venezuela when their revolutions collapsed into dictatorship, all the way back to Chile in 1971. The same people, saying the same empty words, singing the same self-righteous songs from forty years ago, when the world and its challenges were so different. Doing the same thing over and over and expecting a different result.

Forty years in the desert. Nothing. Endless years of nothing, and then suddenly, this. The millennium, from nowhere. They would stop this government and its kangaroo court. The legitimacy of a government lies in the consent of the governed. Wreck the air, the water and the sea in pursuit of profit? Misread the Constitution to arm the forces of repression? Use our hospitals and our nurses and doctors as an excuse to milk us for more tribute? Enslave our young people, turning them all into debtors? There is no state of emergency requiring a recount. You lost fair and square. Now the people speak and you damned well better listen. The sleeping giant has awoken. At last.

Deborah was usually on time. He hurried back to the statue.

She taught him everything he knew. She was five years older than he was, old enough to have gone south in the Civil Rights Movement, old enough for Port Huron, old enough to know the history of the movement and even to have links to the old left. She taught him about music, about who knew who and who slept with whom and who didn't get along, about the friendships and relationships that produced the Summer of Love. She was close to Phil Och's girlfriend. She heard right away about his suicide and went to be with her. Not quite old enough to have been on the bridge at Selma, and certainly not old enough to have been stoned coming through the mob at Beacon or have organized around Emmet Till's murder. But she knew about all of it, and laid it all out for him - stories, ideas, principles, failures and hopes.

He was nobody, just a kid walking into Lowe Library after a snowfall, barely surviving Physics for Poets and way over his head reading Horace and Catullus in Latin, and Homer in Greek. What was he thinking? He could barely form English sentences. He knew about William Carlos Williams and that made him think he could read the classics and write poems? Deborah, on the other hand, was a woman who had lived, who knew people, knew the world, knew what was possible and what was just dreaming, just people believing their own propaganda.

She was building a snow emperor on the steps of the library, her little bit of political theater, a way to be alive after eight inches of snow when everyone else buttoned up their coats and walked with their heads down, afraid to fall.

He helped. He lived in the East Village. So did she. They took the subway home together. The rest is history.

The distance between liking and loving is a sea of unfathomable depth. It's not logical, it's not fair, or kind or decent -- and it's undeniable. Unavoidable. You can't go over it. You can't go under it. You can ignore it, or try to. But it's always there. He liked Deborah. He learned from her, every day. She laughed at his jokes. She listened when he told stories or dissected ideas. She did good work, first at a community center in Harlem while she was in graduate school. Then at a sweat equity housing group in the South Bronx, totally righteous and very Mau Mau, a bunch of Puerto Rican and African-American street kids who occupied abandoned property and taught themselves the trades as they renovated. Solar energy on the roofs. Composting bids and fish ponds in the basements. She ran their VISTA program and coordinated government relations, so she was a kind of big shot there, and kind of a big shot around the city. And he was just a kid, a student, a half-assed writer in the mornings, a cab driver at night, a dreamer. He felt her awkwardness, her secret discomfort around people, her secretiveness, even with him. Her laughter, at jokes, in the movies, was faked, produced, even staged, as if she was acting, timed when others were laughing so she could be part of the herd. He knew she was always ashamed. Many of the feelings she expressed – worry, concern, even righteous indignation, were studied as well, emotions that were designed to look a certain way, to project a certain image, reflect a specific kind of political position.

And he knew that her reach was bigger than her grasp, that she didn't understand much of what she was doing as she was doing it, or why. She was also secretly ashamed of him and of their relationship. He was five years younger. She had the right to love who she loved. But she knew in her heart that no one in her family or among her friends thought he was right for her, that they all thought she stayed with him out of her own insecurity, that she wanted someone weaker than she was, someone willing to be dependent on her.

And that was why, perhaps, he didn't love her after all. He wasn't actually weaker, he was stronger. He felt indulged, even patronized, true, but even more he didn't respect her because he knew she never told herself the truth. She needed someone she could indulge, someone she could objectify. She didn't want to see him as he was, and she wasn't able to listen, not really. He needed someone who actually knew the person he was.

Or that was what he told himself after she walked away. When she told herself the truth that Roland kept evading. That she loved him in fact. But that Roland didn't really love her.

Under the statue of Columbus. Would he recognize Deborah after all these years? The hot dog vendors were there under yellow and blue umbrellas, along with the new and improved pushcarts, the ones that had brilliant white, blue, yellow and green neon signs, that were motorized so they didn't really need to be pushed, and sold all sorts of hallal street food – kabobs, shwarma, even corn dogs and ice cream. There were all sorts of vendors, hustling to make a buck: sellers of posters and watercolors, tee shirts, balloons, counterfeit Gucci bags and hats and scarves of all descriptions. Three or four of them even had commemorative tee-shirts about the General Strike that pictured a throng of people clustered around an upraised red fist, as if the strike was a football team or a rock concert.

The Deborah he'd lost had been thin, dark and precise – dark brown shoulder-length hair, dark brown eyes that never looked quite at you, olive skin, no makeup, ever, and a broad, open face with high cheekbones. She looked more like a folksinger than she did an administrator. She dressed in jeans and a plaid shirt, but looked even better in a slinky black dress, which she wore only when she had to but took off as soon as she could, as if she was never comfortable with her body or any part of the physical world.

How had time changed her? Roland barely recognized himself in the mirror. His hair was thin and grey and he kept it short now, where before he wore it in a ponytail. His big flowing beard was gone. Now there was just a moustache. The thin shoulders and pale skin of his cloistered, bookish youth had been replaced by a sturdy, squat weathered old man, the result of years in the woods, digging fence-posts and dropping logs, but he hunched over some. He thought he looked like a gnome, where he had been tall and thin as a young man. Would she know him? What would it be like to be with her again for an afternoon? Would they still have a connection? Once, she had been a part of him: he really knew her, and she had known him, as much as she was able to know anyone. Was that still there, or would they be strangers, catching up on different lives, narrating the story as if reading from a book?

Roland heard the clop and clatter of hooves on pavement and spun around. Twenty police officers on big bay horses trotted on the Park Drive south, one long block away, above the throng and just visible through the still leafless trees. People shouted as they rushed to get out of the way. The officers sat erect on their horses. Their black helmets glistened in the late morning sun, their blue jackets a strange cloud moving low across the park, a school of fish or a flock of birds swimming or flying together as one. That's a little weird, Roland thought. Mounted police? I thought the deal was very limited police presence, that the march and the strike had the full support of the Mayor and the Governor as well. Solidarity. Painfully but finally achieved, after this democracy had looked the chaos and disaster of fascism in the face and had backed away from that. The consent of the governed. The people united will never be defeated. One nation indivisible, the whole so much greater than the sum of the parts. He started to do the math, to play strategist again, to think about the end game, the way his mind used to work on the old days. If there are mounted police here and they are moving south, his brain said, what's happening in Lower East Side and at the convention center, where there is room for twenty or thirty thousand police?

"Roland," Deborah said, and he turned around.

"Yeah," he said.

And there she was, the woman herself.

Not much different. He held her at arm's length so they could look at one another. Then he pulled her to him and she reach up and wrapped her hands around the back of his neck they way she used to do, forty years before.

Deborah was still tall for a woman. She had the same red-framed glasses and the same worried expression, intense and a little confused at the same time, the same brown eyes that looked lost and worried, always searching for approval and unconditional love, the same broad, open forehead and brow that knit easily when she was thinking. But her brown hair was tinged with grey, her eyebrows had become grey and the skin over her cheekbones had become wrinkled and flaccid where it had once been taught and smooth. The skin on her neck was now fleshy and wrinkled, like the skin of an old woman.

But Deborah wasn't an old woman. She was Deborah, the same person she used to be. She backed away, looked at him again for a moment, up and down, and then hugged him to her again, holding him as tightly as she could.

"What happened to us?" she said, and sobbed, and then strangely, uncomfortably, Roland's throat closed, he was unable to speak, and his eyes were wet even though it wasn't raining.

Then something pushed Roland backward. A shock wave. A wall of sound so loud that people bent over in the street to get away from it.

Sirens. Sirens everywhere, piercing and painful, that pushed him and pushed Deborah, a fierce wind that flattened his skin and his eyes. New York sirens, WHANWAN WHANWAN, WHANWAN, WHANWAN, in and out, whopping and burning, designed to wake the dead, beat the living into submission, to cut through glass and empty streets jammed with traffic to make way for any vehicle that had its siren blaring. But there wasn't one siren or one vehicle. There were hundreds. Police cars and police vans which had been parked on the cross streets and avenues had suddenly come to life.

Suddenly it was impossible to move and or to think. Roland couldn't hear. Deborah tried to speak but stopped after a word or two. She couldn't hear her own voice. How naïve they all were. Four million people in the street. Did anyone really believe that the forces of reaction, the dark side of the force, would just shrink into a ball and roll away? The other side, those forces of reaction, they were no more than twenty or thirty million people, less than ten percent of the nation -- but they had three hundred and fifty million guns. They'd had their four years, and power, once tasted, is a drug like cocaine, a wild high that once you rode up never wants to let you down.

"Let's get the hell out of here," Roland shouted. And then he realized he couldn't hear himself either. So he gestured. And then he opened his coat and wrapped Deborah's head in it to cushion her ears, and pushed her down the stairs into the subway, through ten thousand other people who were coming up the stairs, because someone needed to survive this day, and now anything and everything was possible, none of it good, and most of it likely too painful to bear. There would be tear gas, gunfire, a sky filled with drones and pandemonium in the streets.

"Stop," Deborah said, as soon as they could hear one another speak, when they were half-way down the staircase and surrounded by people. "I'm not going to let you run away again."

"What?" Roland said. "I haven't seen you in 40 years. You want to have an argument already?"

"No argument. No discussion. You can do whatever you want. I'm going back up to join the demonstration," Deborah said.

"It's a mess out there," Roland said.

"But it's our mess," Deborah said. "Running away isn't going to change that."

"People are going to get killed out there," Roland said.

"People get killed out there every day. You can live on your knees. Or die on your feet. There are four million people on the street. We're old. And everyone dies of something. There is nothing to fear but fear itself," Deborah said. She turned and walked up the stairs, disappearing into the crowd of thousands.

Stunned. Roland was stunned. Nothing like this had ever happened to him before. It was like someone had hit him over the head with a club, like he had been knocked unconscious. But he was still standing. The subway staircase was cold and dark because the sunlight hadn't penetrated here. There were a zillion people pushing their way up the stairs. And Roland was in their way, standing there like a lost sheep, not entirely sure where he was, what he was doing or where he was going.

Someone needs to survive this mess, he said to himself again, hearing the sirens in his brain and seeing pictures of armed men in uniforms and carrying Plexiglas shields, pushing the crowd back in his imagination. He saw pictures in his mind of drones firing on the crowd and clouds of tear gas. He felt the sting of mace in his eyes, and felt himself gasping for breath, felt himself pouring gallons and gallons of water over his face to make the burning stop. It felt real to him, a present danger. Even though none of that had happened to him, and Roland had no idea what was actually happening in the street.

He stumbled down the stairs, forcing his way through the crowd by sticking close to one wall and holding on to the handrail. The handrail was cold and covered with layers of old soft blue paint, which peeled off as his fingernails dug into it. Then he fought his way to the platform. Uptown. He needed to go uptown. His car was in the Bronx. He needed to get away from this madness. Someone needed to survive.

The uptown platform was deserted. A train rolled in, packed to the windows with people, who streamed out the minute the doors opened, the people nearest the doors stumbling out, propelled by the force of the huge throng behind them. Roland stood behind a pillar until there was space for him to move. Then he maneuvered his way into the subway car, just before the doors closed. Stand clear of the closing doors, please, the voice over the loudspeaker said.

But there was no need for that announcement. There was no one on the train but Roland.

The doors closed and the train started to move. Roland was alone. Deborah and come and gone in an instant, and was now likely lost forever. There was likely to be a maelstrom happening just over his head, on the streets the train ran beneath.

The doors opened at 79th Street. There was no one on the platform. The subway station was empty.

Roland walked off the train. He stood for a moment. There was a rush of air, a cold wind, and then the flash of the headlight of a southbound train.

The doors of the train Roland had just come off closed.

The southbound train roared and shook its way into the station, packed with people and their rowdy doomed lives. Live on your knees or die on your feet. Live forever on your own, or be part of what's bigger than you are, however doomed or misguided. No one lives forever.

There is only one life.

Roland pushed his way into the throng of people on the southbound train, alive and dying, standing clear of the closing doors at last.

The Choke Artist

You're a choke artist. You're useless. Insubstantial. Impotent. Meaningless. Weak.

The choke artist is a man or woman but almost always a man who can't perform under pressure. Under pressure, the choke artist gets anxious, chokes up, and can't deliver. Can't catch the football when the crowd is cheering and the chips are down. Can't hit the baseball at the bottom of the ninth when bases are loaded. Can't swim the Bosporus in the middle of the summer during a revolution and can't get it up to make love to the woman of his dreams who is standing on the other side. Loses his nerve, doesn't go for the jugular, gets beat on the deal. Has thoughts. Emotions. A two pump Charlie. Chokes up at movies when love or justice triumphs, when the hero finds himself or herself in the other. Doesn't win at poker. Doesn't sacrifice the other in the service of the self. We are Achilles. Hector is a choke artist, one of the tens of thousands who were destroyed by Achilles and his hot anger, their souls thrown down to Sheol because they choked.

A choke artist is not a hunger artist. A hunger artist gets attention by starving himself in public. He appeals to our unconscious fascination with the plight of others who are suffering, who also say to themselves, "better him than me." How long will the hunger artist last? How will he weaken? How will he die? The hunger artist makes his living by dying on the installment plan and by inviting the throng to his slow, excruciating death. We experience the pathos of his death which is our life and death: the only way to find love is to consume the self. The throng grows larger when the panther comes into the hunger artist's cage. The hunger artist succeeds when millions of people come out to watch the panther tear him limb from limb, and watch the panther devour his entrails, red blood coating the panther's black muzzle. That's the reality. Reality TV. We thrill as the panther licks his chops. Who's next?

But the choke artist just fails to act and then just fails, and is kicked off the wagon and left to die alone by the side of the road. Then someone else calls his failure to our attention. We delight in not being him, in being anonymous and not a failure, or not having our failures noticed, at least not right then. We discover that others delight in not being him as well, and so a larger self, a crowd, a mob, a mass is built out of all of us who delight in the failure of others. Someone does this to and with us. Someone acts to create a larger self for us by un-roofing our base instincts, by preying on that hidden part of our psyche. We are easily led, a stiff-necked people, idol worshipers and lovers of Baal. We love to mock the weak. Someone loves to call attention to the choke artist's failure which is not our failure. Someone uses our weakness to build a mob that rises when we don't or can't see the weakness in ourselves.

Them people come into our yard on Superbowl Sunday.

They talk Spanish or whatever and who the hell knows what they're saying. They could be ISIS or terrorists. The Christmas lights is still up and now I got a sign up too. Super Bowl Sunday. I am watching the pregame and Maureen is on that computer, shopping and whatnot.

There are two of them, one greasier than the next.

One is short and built like a tank, big eyebrows and big ears and a moustache and a little goatee and a buzz-cut like he just got out of the joint and the other is little and skinny with tiny little ears and beady eyes wearing an army surplus jacket and also with a buzz-cut like they are thugs or gangbangers or whatever and they are driving this beat up old pickup with the side panels all rusted out. No self respecting American would drive a truck like that.

I am watching Mr. Tom Brady choke up and thinking about Donald J. Trump and all that he is saying. I didn't get Mr. Trump at first with his talk about people who choke up. I get 'You're Fired' but I don't get the choke artist stuff. He has balls, that Donald J. Trump. He called out George W. Bush, that wimp, and even John McCain who is a whiner and Trump ain't afraid to live large so I put up the yard sign but I don't get the choke artist stuff yet.

That Trump ain't afraid of much. But suddenly when I see the Spanish drive up I get what Donald J. Trump is about. We need people who can perform, who will defend us, defend me and my way of life, who aren't afraid and who just don't quit.

The Spanish and the immigrants and the terrorists come into our country and we let them in and before long they are coming into our yard on Super Bowl Sunday and they are taking over. And this country isn't for us any more, it is for them. If they can just walk right up today, they can walk right up at Christmas or any day they want. Somebody let them in. That somebody also let all the good jobs go to Mexico. We had textiles and carpets and lawnmowers and we had costume jewelry and we had plastics and steel and machine tools and now that's all picked up and moved to Mexico, to China, to Thailand, to Bangladesh and Brazil, you name it. Whatever we had is packed up and gone. The rich get richer and the rest of us get screwed. They say go to school but shit, you can't nary get into one of them colleges. Them colleges is for rich people's kids only, and if you do get in they charge you an arm and a fucking leg and their loans keep you bound and gagged until you're sixty and like to die. Once upon a time you'd get four percent on your money in the bank and a house loan would cost you five percent. Now you get nothing in the bank, and maybe a house loan cost four percent but the houses ain't worth shit no more so you owe more than house is worth and now the jobs is gone and you gotta work two crappy jobs to pay down the loan but you ain't never going to get anything for that house anyway. The fix is in. Them Wall Street bankers get paid but we get screwed. And with this Obamacare now you can get insurance but the insurance costs more than a house loan and it don't cover shit so when you go to the doctor they still charge you an arm and a leg and they still sit behind them sliding glass windows and all they care about is your co-pay which is now more than a doctor's visit used to cost and now they won't give you no medicine if your back hurts or if you got the headache. They hide behind too many drug overdoses and shit. They got rules and forms and reasons but we the people who built this country and we the people who died for it, we keep getting screwed.

We got a blow-up Santa in the yard and three of them light-up reindeers, the ones that move their heads back and forth, back and forth. I got myself a yard sign that is half as big as the house and I am flying a big old American flag right over it and I have red white and blue Christmas lights laid over the bushes and wrapped around the house.

Anyhow these boys come into the yard. I'm in the living room, watching the Broncos kick the ass of the New England Patriots. That high and mighty Mr. Tom Brady had it coming. I'm in the living room and I see the truck pull up and these boys get out, come into my yard and start to come up my drive. I see them out of the bay window in the condo and I am thinking, choke artist, choke artist, choke artist.

The hunger artist acts by withholding action. The choke artist only chokes. The hunger artist has an art to what he does, a perverse skill. But there is no art of the choke. The choking person just chokes up and then someone else who has something to sell mocks him or her and turns us away from his own failings and from the failure which he suggests he will avoid because he isn't afraid to mock the weak. I am better than that, he says. Because he speaks, we believe him, because we are easily led and weak ourselves, a weakness we don't feel as long as someone mocks the other, or we mock the other ourselves.

This is not a story about art. Art excites the imagination so we see ourselves in the other, so we see how the other sees and feel how the other feels. Art is intentional. Art is light. Not mockery.

Which means the choke artist not an artist after all. He's a sub-artist or an anti-artist, a man who fails to do what he knows how to do. Or perhaps doesn't know how to do. We never find out if he's any good because he chokes up.

The architect of the choke, on the other hand, is able to feast on the livers of the damned. He can make a man or a woman choke so you can laugh at them. Lots of ways to do that. Let the chokee know you know what he's secretly terrified of and make that public. You are too small, too big, too smart, too dumb, too dishonest, too rigidly honest, too awkward. You'll see the chokee stand up straight and start to sweat when you hit the soft spot, so watch out of the corner of your eye. Mock his mother. Threaten his kid. He loves. He's vulnerable. Move in for the kill.

The architect of the choke is the sleuth of the unconscious and the maestro of fear, the man who can find the fears you keep hidden from yourself and who can make you believe that what you are afraid of is what is about to happen, so you focus on the fear and not on the task at hand. The architect of the choke cuts off the air of mindfulness, the air that the mind breathes as it stands in the present moment. The architect of the choke deflects your attention from him to you as he deflects our attention from you to him, and with the same sleight of hand submerges his own character so all we see about him is that he just beat you – we don't see how and we don't see who and we don't see why. All we see is that you are weak. Even when you're not.

There are other chokes and other architects. We say grow tomatoes and give you a loan to build greenhouses, which you do. The bottom drops out of the market. You can't pay the loan. Choking, you sell your land. We say, here's a cool device which your kids will love. You love your kids, you buy the device, the kids use the device and you never see them again. You choke on your love. We say you need school to be successful. School is expensive. Take a loan. You take a loan, go to school but never find a job. Choke on the loan. Or you do find a job and you do pay back the loan but now you can't afford a spouse or a house or a car or kids, so you have a loan but no love. Choke on the loan again. He says he loves you so you sell your house and move west, and then he loves you and three or four others. Choke on love.

I'm on it. I yell to Maureen, call 911 we got trouble, and I reach into the hall closet where my little surprise lives in its little box on the highest shelf in the back. My little .357 surprise has been waiting for something like this. My insurance policy. My ticket to ride. This is what I got her for. I pull her out and pop her into the waistband of my camouflage pants behind my back where you can't see her and I have the front door open before those boys get past the bushes at the bottom of the walk. After I got laid off from the carpet plant I used to restore cars before I got disabled from the back pain and the neuropathy and a bad heart, but I'm still pretty quick.

I open the door and stand out on the porch.

"You boys stop where you are," I say.

"We no fear," the stocky one says.

"Looking work," the little one says. "You got work? We got truck. Mower. Chain saw. We clean basement. Yard work. Shovel snow. Whatever. We good work."

"You stop where you are, turn yourselves around, get in that truck and take yourselves back to wherever the hell you came from," I say.

"Good work," the stocky one says. "We good work."

"Get the hell out of my yard," I say, and I start to come down the steps. 'This is private property." My voice is loud now.

Them two boys look at one another like they never seen a man stand his ground. My neighbor who himself is a Spanish guy hears us and comes out on his porch. He himself is Spanish but he is American, by which I mean he was born here and speaks normal. Teacher by day. Security guard by night.

"This is private property," I say.

"No trouble," the stocky guy says.

Two or three other neighbors come out of their houses. Julio the teacher picks up a baseball bat and walks off his porch. The Spanish guys start to back away.

"You Trump?" the little guy says, and he grins, a smartass.

"Yeah Trump," I say, and I pull the gun out of my waistband. "Make America great again."

They talk, we listen. They must think we're all stupid. Because we are. We let them talk and we listen as if we are learning something but they are always exactly the same and we let ourselves choose one over the other, distracted by the spectacle as they steal our patrimony and set us against one another. We love the thrill of people fighting, the way kids in the schoolyard thrill to watch the bully taunt the weak kid or the different kid or just any kid. They keep testing our unconscious fear, sniffing our nether regions, searching for a smell everyone else can smell or a weakness everyone else can see or they invent one, conjurers that they are, and see if they can get the kids on the schoolyard to suspend their disbelief and ride with them, imagine with them, and then they ride that thermal of a rumor or a myth, ride the ugly wind of the collective voice, rising in their own minds above the earth. We elect them or crown them or obey them – and they go and cut deals, using the public space and the illusion of their power to make themselves rich. We are stupid to believe them, and yet we do, over and over again. They are the choke architect and the lie artist and the mirage artist. They colonize our uncertainties, doubts and fears.

We gather and we thrill. Eventually, we choke or are choked, as the architect of the choke turns to us. First we choke on our own weakness. Then we consume ourselves, digesting our own flesh to stay alive. The panther comes into the cage.

That .357 changes the equation. I hold it in front of me, pointing it at the stocky one who backs off behind a bush.

The other neighbors start to come off their porches and the two Spanish guys back away more, keeping their eyes on me.

I hear sirens in the distance. Them sirens is still far away but they is coming closer. Too bad I told Maureen to call the cops.

"Asshole," the little one says. "Trump asshole."

Whatever you think of Donald J. Trump it is just not smart to come on a man's property and insult him, particularly if that man is holding a firearm. I am at the bottom of the stairs and I walk forward towards those assholes. Julio starts to come across the grass between our houses. Other people come down from their porches.

"Fuck you," I say. The stocky one is half behind the shrub at the bottom of the driveway. I don't have a clean shot. I draw a bead on the little one. But he's a fast bugger and he drops behind the Ram which is parked next to the house.

The sirens are close.

I advance. Fuck them all.

The first cop drives up fast. He is big and Black and he turns off his siren as he pulls up but leaves the lights flashing. Then there is a second and a third and they drive right up on the grass or leave their cars at angles kitty-cornered in the street, blocking it. There are five or six cops and five or six cop cars.

Two or three of them cops are Black or Spanish. Isn't that a nice how do you do?

They have their guns drawn.

And those guns are pointing at me.

"Drop the weapon," the Black cop says. I look for the Spanish guys. I didn't know one of them had a weapon.

Then suddenly it hits me. The guns are pointed at me. The Black cop is talking to me. To him I am the perp. Holy fuck. All at once I start to see the whole thing like it's on television, shot from the perspective of a cameraman in a helicopter hovering just over my head.

"It's them," I say, to the cop, as I turn towards him. "They're the trouble. I live here. I'm the American here. I'm the good guy."

"Drop the gun. Drop the gun. Drop the fucking gun," the Black cop says.

For an instant, I hear the voice of the TV reporter who exists only in my head. "Wilmington man was gunned down by police after a standoff that involved two hostages," the voice says, and I think, holy shit, that Wilmington man is me. Goddamn cops, my brain says, maybe I should take one or two of them with me, I've had it up to here. But then my gut takes over from my brain, and I throw the gun down and hit the deck.

Then they are all over me, my arms pinned behind my back, a nightstick under my neck. Big white guy on top of me, huffing and puffing. They are too damn big for me, those cops. The Black cop stands off to the side like he is in charge.

"Watch my back. Watch my fucking back," I say. "I've got a bad back. And neuropathy. And a bad heart."

The choke artist is pinned on the ground, his hands pulled behind his back, a night stick jammed against his trachea, gasping. I can't breathe, he says.

And then he dies.

Goddamn it's hard some days to respect the law and remember that the Constitution says citizen have rights, even dumbass citizens who wave guns around in the late afternoon at the end of January. Life, liberty and the pursuit of happiness. I'm not seeing how there is a right to wave a .357 Magnum around like it is a red white and blue pinwheel on the Fourth of July.

My guys have emotions too. They don't love having weapons pointed at them. Don't love is an understatement. They get hyped and they overdo it when they get hyped. Tempting as it is to let the little white guy suffer, I call off the dogs.

"Stand down," I shout. "Book him, don't strangle him. Just because he's an idiot doesn't mean you have to be idiots as well."

You give these little white guys guns and they think they are the masters of the universe. They think they can do what they want and that they can say what they want and that the law doesn't apply to them. Second Amendment my ass. The last thing this country needed was to put .357 Magnums, AR-15s and Uzis and into the hands of Joe Six-pack.

I'm the police. I'm also a Black man in America. I think, for a moment, about my own people, who never get the time of day. Not from the police, not even from my police, not from anybody. If this guy had been Black, you know and I know and my guys know that the little white guy would have had five holes in him before he hit the ground. It's all out of control. Out of everyone's control. Unless we take it back.

The cop stands, leaving the night stick on the ground, and rubs his hands together, a dead man at his feet. Who is the artist? What do we know about the hunger artist who died and the choke artist left behind? See the power of words. See words run. See words choke. See Spot choke on words. See us use our words. The Wall Street bankers and the venture capitalists and Federal Government use their words to take everything from us, even human dignity, even compassion, which all got sacrificed to a twenty percent return. When was the last time you heard a human being answer a telephone? Words come from the automated attendant but they aren't real words with real meanings because there is no person on the other end, speaking them. Language has meaning only when two people talk to one another. They don't even have human beings at the checkout counters of the supermarket anymore.

Thank God the choke artist didn't die. The little white guy lay there gasping for breath. His throat and neck was going to be seriously sore in the morning. "I can't breathe," he gasped. But he could breathe, this time. I used my better judgment and we let him live. There has to be some common ground left, some place for us to be together as human beings. The ambulance rolled up, its lights even brighter than the lights of the squad cars, the red blue and bright white light bathing all of us in strange colors and shadows in the late afternoon.

Who is the choke artist? Are our lives real or are they just art? Have we all been reduced to pederasty?

The architect of the choke is the Music Man and Darth Vader, Hitler and Jesus and Lucifer and Buddha and Moses and Mohammed and Mick Jaeger and Paul McCartney, all rolled into one. Nothing happens until somebody sells something. The architect of the choke is choker and chokee at once. We all need someone to bleed on. And you know if you want it, you can bleed on me.

The Black cop must have had second thoughts, and he and another cop pulled that mad dog off me. I must have blacked out. I wake up gasping, my throat closed, my head ready to explode. But then the light came back and I could see them all standing around me. They cuffed me and rolled me over. Then they lifted me, one guy on each side of me. Then Rescue rolled up and they put me in it.

"Get him checked out before we book him," the Black cop said. "Mister," he said to me, "don't you ever do like that again. Call 911. Don't be waving a goddamn gun around your neighborhood on a Sunday afternoon. You coulda got three people killed."

"They came onto my property," I said. "I got rights."

"I don't care if they came into your goddamn bedroom while you were fucking your wife's sister," the Black cop said. "Dead men don't pursue happiness. Just call 911 and leave the weaponry to us please."

The artist is always an actor, someone who does. The choked is forced into inaction, so stuck he or she can't even move air into his or her chest. And then he dies. Democracy is for the living. We are a society made of actors, who interact. The architect of the choke locks us down, so we don't move. He takes our love, our compassion, our decency, and he monetizes it and then weaponizes it. He calls us a choke artist, a wimp, weak, small, white, black, yellow, a loser, so that we choke. He sells us what we don't want and don't need and then we choke. He thinks he is laughing, all the way to the bank. And he is not alone. He is just one incarnation of the evil impulse. He and his brothers and sisters in crime are out there sucking up all the air we breathe. Which is the air they breathe. Just sayin.

Art awakens the imagination so that we see who we are and who we can be together. The architect of the choke exploits the imagination in the service of his ego and his greed and he will destroy us all to feed himself. Lucifer. Nero. Stalin. Hitler. Caesar. Sabbati Zevi. Caligula. The dark side of the force. The black hole. The destroyer. The Dark Lord of the Sith. This isn't science fiction. It's our life, our experience. Give us this day our daily bread.

Man is born free but is everywhere enslaved. Workers unite, you have nothing to lose but your chains. Chain chain chain, chain of fools.

If we don't stand up for democracy we will lose it. The people who choke are the people who will die. Only the people who stand up together and act up together will live.

Now is the time for all good men to come to the aid of their country. And women. And everyone else, left and right, up and down and in-between.

Democracy is the air we breathe. The choke artist is standing on our collective neck.

It's time to stand up together and get this monkey off our back. And all them other monkeys with him.

No justice, no peace.

Kick out the jams.

Awaking Horse

She was a beautiful cream color, with a white tail and mane, a mare, and we remembered her blue eyes from before she fell asleep. We had great hopes for her. We would use her to take milk from the cows and goats to market, and also take the vegetables that we grew on the farm in the spring and summer and the split wood in the winter. That way there would be the money we needed to buy more animals and more land, and perhaps enough to build a bigger barn for more cows, and a bigger house. Then we might buy a carriage, and make a little more money yet, transporting our neighbors to the city, from time to time, or to the train station, or to see their families who lived just a little too far off to walk.

But it all came to nothing. One day my father brought her back from the fair, where they buy and sell horses in a field outside the city once a month in the spring and summer at the full moon. Our father was riding on her bare back, and she was prancing, her head held high. We all came out of the house to see this horse and we all looked at her with astonishment and delight because she was so beautiful, and because she was ours. Then we took turns riding on her broad back. Our father boosted us up, lifting each of us in turn by the armpits so we could throw one leg over her back and wrap our hands in her white mane, the hairs as thick as string and as strong as wood. Our father led her around the courtyard front of the house, and we each giggled or screeched with delight as we rode, holding on to her mane so that we didn't fall off. When our father tired, he let me lead, and the new cream-colored horse stood patiently as the rest of us helped the next child to clamber up on the cream-colored horse's back. One of us went on hands and knees to let that child stand on our backs, and then we boosted that child with our hands wrapped together to hold their feet so we could lift them. Then we let that child put her or his feet on our shoulders as they rose higher and higher next to the patient horse's back, until the lifted child was high enough to throw one foot over the horse's back and sit upright, their hands entwined into the cream-colored horse's white mane.

Children love with their whole souls, with abandon, and we loved the cream-colored horse in that way. We loved her so much that we all dreamed about her, and we took turns telling our dreams. Our father cleared a stall in the barn of old furniture and broken farm implements, and we decorated it with flowers, pine branches and herbs, so the home of our cream colored horse would look as pretty as she looked and would always smell fresh and clean. None of us could imagine a better life.

But a few weeks later the horse fell asleep.

She didn't die. She just didn't wake up.

She lay on her side in her stall. She didn't move except to breathe, and her breathing was slow and heavy, as if she were dreaming heavy dreams of sadness or worry, or remembering what she had loved and lost. Her stall smelled of vanilla at night and of the rich warm fetid smell of manure and horse urine in the mornings. Sometimes her tail switched in her sleep, as if she was dreaming about a pasture where the grass was long and green, the sun was strong, and there were insects flitting about in the then warm sunlight.

We thought she would die, at first, and a gloom descended on our household as thick as the sadness and despair we would have felt if one of us were dying, or if the country had gone to war. We didn't play in the house any more. When we played outside, we went far from the house and played quietly so as not to wake the horse. Our father brought men to look at the horse but they all went away shaking their heads. They had never seen anything like it and not one of them knew what to do. Soon people began to avoid us, as if afraid that what had befallen our beautiful horse, and us, would also befall their horses and their families and loved ones.

And yet the horse lived. Every day we brought hay and water, and left it in the stall. Every morning, the hay and water were gone and there was a pile of manure in the corner of the stall. None of us ever saw her awake and stand. Her living and sleeping was a great mystery, a question for which we had no answer.

And so we lived in the shadow of her sleeping. There was no horse to pull the cart to market, and no money to do the things we had been dreaming of. There was no horse to ride at twilight in the courtyard of our house, no way for us to take turns scrambling on her back and leading her in circles. We were left with the life we always had. We tried not to think about the horse or the dreams she had let us dream. She lay in the stall in a dark corner of the barn and we never went there other than to bring her hay and water and to muck out her stall. The flowers in her stall wilted, the herbs dried, and the branches we put there lost their needles and fell from the walls. The barn became a dark place that we all tried to avoid.

Eighteen months came and went. There was, in fact, a war. Young men donned uniforms, and talked bravely about battles and guns and how the enemy was very fierce and very evil. They knew they would be brave and that the enemy would be vanquished. But when they went away, only a few came back. We heard about others, who languished in hospitals in distant places, having been disfigured or maimed, and that made us very sad indeed. We were too young for the war, but we also counted the years -- if the war went on too long, I would have to go and that worried me, because I was not bold, not wont to see another people as the enemy, and not certain that battles or the slaughter of human beings could awaken the horse or solve the problems we had on our farm, with our neighbors, or in the cities nearby.

They called our father to go to war, and we were afraid and very sad indeed. I was old enough and my sisters and brother were old enough to feed the cows and the goats and bring in the hay.

In that moment our childhood ended. We worked hard in the fields or tending to the cattle and goats whenever we weren't in school. Our hearts stayed hidden, and our thoughts were always clouded over in that time, worried about our father, sad about the horse, empty because of the war, and hoping only that time would pass and that the world could right itself, so we could go back to laughing together, to clamoring up the horse's back and leading her around the courtyard, shrieking with delight.

All this time the horse lay on her side all day long, breathing heavily and deeply asleep. We tried not to think about her.

One day our father came home from the war wearing a tattered uniform. He was unhurt on the outside. But now he was silent. A certain weight was lifted off our backs, but our old life did not return. Our father went back to work in the fields, but he shut himself up in his room at night, and was short with us, where before he had been so warm and loving. We did not permit ourselves to dream.

And then one day we heard a whinny. The horse! We went running to her stall. She still lay on her side but her eyes opened for a moment. The smell of her was different. There was a new smell about her -- a rich, languid smell, the smell of orchids and of pollens.

Then, for a few days, we heard snores and coughs from the horse's stall. She was still asleep, but sometimes her eyes opened for a moment at a time. One of our sisters said she thought our mare was in heat.

Three days later, just before dawn, we heard whinnying, not once or twice, but one call after the next, as if our horse was alive again and was whistling a tune, so loud and clear it felt like we were dreaming again. We shook ourselves out of our slumber and our warm beds and went running to the barn. It was a cold clear morning, and the long yellow rays of first sun angled through the bare trees across the courtyard. The birds had come back and were calling to one another as they flitted from place to place, and the chickens in the yard had clustered about, waiting to be fed.

The horse was awake and standing on her feet. Her eyes were dull, as if she wasn't fully awake yet, but great clouds of steam flowed from her nostrils as her warm moist breath flowed into the crisp morning air. It was unbelievable. She blinked as if she didn't quite recognize where she was or why she was here, or even what she wanted yet. But she was awake and she was standing on her own.

We crowded around her, wanting nothing more than to touch her warm flanks, to pet her warm strong neck, or to touch the soft spots around her mouth and nostrils, which were black in color and as soft and warm as porridge.

Then our father came and shooed us away. He stood silent and looked at the horse, face to face, his breathing also making tiny clouds in the crisp morning air. Horses don't look you in the eye the way a person does. There isn't the same fix and focus. They take you in as part of the scenery, as one tiny perceptual fact in a broad bright world of colors and shapes, which they see themselves as part of without perceiving self and other as we perceive it, as if time and nature are part of one continuum, as if there is no future, no past and no memory and no hope of change but only the strange threatening majesty of the present.

I don't know what our father expected to learn from the horse. Perhaps he only wanted to know if he could trust her to remain standing and awake, to find out if she who had disappointed him and us so intensely could ever be trusted with his and our hopes again.

It didn't matter. He reached out and patted her nose. Then he went into the kitchen, and made her a mash of warm milk, oats and molasses which he brought out to her in a bucket and which she hungrily and enthusiastically consumed, licking the corners of the bucket with her tongue to sop up every drop, as if she were a cow.

And then our father put a rope halter around her head, and led her out into the courtyard, into the sunlight. The cream-colored horse walked gingerly, slowly, as if she wasn't sure of the location of her feet, and when she came out of the barn she blinked and appeared dazed. But she followed our father diligently, not sure of herself but trusting him, the rope that tugged on her muzzle guiding her gently forward.

Our father found a second lead rope in the paddock and clipped it to her halter. He passed each lead rope around a different side of her neck so he had reins with which to steer her. Then he got up on a mounting block and leapt onto her back.

All of a sudden, the old cream-colored horse we knew, the horse we hoped for and loved, was returned to us. The horse held her head high again. The brightness came back to her eyes. She trotted out of the courtyard, lifting her feet high, almost prancing.

Our father came back two days later, leading the horse. He put her back into her stall, which we decorated again with flowers and herbs and pine branches, and he brought her mash every morning, mash he made himself, and he patted her neck as she ate it. He pulled an old horse cart that lay covered with dust and cobwebs from the corner of the barn, painted it bright orange, and began to bring milk, butter, and cheese to market once a week. Before he set out, we covered the cart in flowers, and wove flowers into the cream colored horse's mane and tail.

A year later, when we had almost forgotten our long period of sadness while the horse slept, we heard a whinny in the night, and then a second whinny and then a small high pitched snort and a very weak cough. We all jumped out of bed and went running out to the barn. By lamp light we saw the new foal still wet from her mother's womb. The foal was jet black and struggling to stand.

All at once we were in love again.

Now we are the owners of horses. We pamper them with mash and fill their stalls with flowers, because we remember when our horse slept and our lives were without feeling or hope.

About the Author

Michael Fine is a writer, community organizer, family physician, public health official, and author of *Health Care Revolt: How to Organize, Build a Health Care System, and Resuscitate Democracy –All at the Same Time* and *Abundance,* a romantic thriller set in Rhode Island and in Liberia in the aftermath of the Liberian Civil Wars of 1989-2003.

The Bull and Other Stories is his first collection of short stories.

All the stories in *The Bull and Other Stories* are available as a podcast called **Alternative Fictions: New Stories from Michael Fine.** Find the podcast at https://linktr.ee/drmichaelfine.

All of Michael Fine's stories and books are available at www.MichaelFineMD.com

Also by Michael Fine

ABUNDANCE

ISBN: 978162963-644-3

$17.95 • 5x8 •352 pages

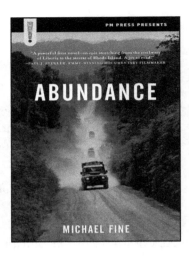

Julia is an American medical doctor fleeing her own privileged background to find a new life delivering health care to African villages, where her skills can make a difference. Carl is also an American, whose very different experiences as a black man in the United States have driven him into exile in West Africa, where he is an international NGO expat. The two come to- gether as colleagues (and then more) as Liberia is gripped in a brutal civil war. Child soldiers kidnap Julia on a remote jungle road, and Carl is evac- uated against his will by U.S. Marines. Back in the United States he finds Julia's mentor, Levin, a Rhode Island MD whose Sixties idealism has been hijacked by history. Then they meet the thief. Then they meet the smuggler. And the dangerous work of finding and rescuing Julia begins.

An unforgettable thriller grounded in real events.

"Michael Fine's novel, *Abundance*, is a riveting, suspenseful tale of love, violence, adventure, idealism, sometimes-comic cynicism, class conflict and crime . . . a story that displays both the deep disconnect between the First and Third Worlds and our commonalities."
>   —Robert Whitcomb, former finance editor of the *International Herald Tribune* and former editorial page editor of the *Providence Journal*

"Michael Fine takes us into the heart of a country at war with itself. But our journey, in battered Land Rovers, along potholed red dirt roads, is pro- pelled by love, not hate. That love offers hope for Liberia, our often forgot- ten sister country, and anyone who confronts despair. Read *Abundance*. Reignite your own search for a life worth living."
>   —Martha Bebinger, WBUR

"A powerful first novel—an epic stretching from the civil wars of Liberia to the streets of Rhode Island. A joy to read!"
>   —Paul J. Stekler, Emmy-winning documentary filmmaker

Also by Michael Fine

HEALTH CARE REVOLT
How to Organize, Build a Health Care System, and Resuscitate Democracy— All at the Same Time

Foreword by Bernard Lown MD and Ariel Lown Lewiton

ISBN: 978162963-581-1

$15.95 • 5.5x8.5 •192 pages

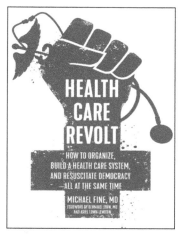

The U.S. does not have a health system. Instead we have market for health- related goods and services, a market in which the few profit from the public's ill-health.

Health Care Revolt looks around the world for examples of health care systems that are effective and affordable, pictures such a system for the U.S., and creates a practical playbook for a political revolution in health care that will allow the nation to protect health while strengthening democracy.

Dr. Fine writes with the wisdom of a clinician, the savvy of a state public health commissioner, the precision of a scholar, and the energy and commitment of a community organizer.

"This is a revolutionary book. The author incites readers to embark on an audacious revolution to convert the American medical market into the American health care system."
    —T.P. Gariepy, Stonehill College/CHOICE connect

"Michael Fine is one of the true heroes of primary care over several decades."
    —Dr. Doug Henley, CEO and executive vice president of the American Academy of Family Physicians

"As Rhode Island's director of health, Dr. Fine brought a vision of a humane, local, integrated health care system that focused as much on health as on disease and treatment."
    —U.S. Senator Sheldon Whitehouse

"Michael Fine has given us an extraordinary biopic on health care in America based on the authority of his forty-year career as writer, community organizer, family physician, and public health official."
    —Fitzhugh Mullan, MD

THE NATURE OF HEALTH

How America lost, and can regain,

a Basic Human Value

Foreword by Robert S. Lawrence M.D.

ISBN: 978036744-619-2

6x9 •264 pages

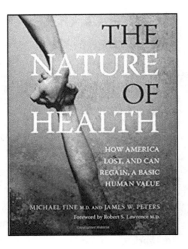

This pioneering work addresses a key issue that confronts all industrialized nations: How do we organize healthcare services in accordance with fundamental human rights, whilst competing with scientific and technological advances, powerful commercial interests and widespread public ignorance?

The Nature of Health presents a coherent, affordable and logical way to build a healthcare system. It argues against a health system fixated on the pursuit of longevity and suggests an alternative where the ability of an individual to function in worthwhile relationships is a better, more human goal.

By reviewing the etymology, sociology and anthropology of health, this controversial guide examines the meaning of health, and proves how a community-centered healthcare system improves local economy, creates social capital and is affordable, rational, personal, and just.

"This is badly needed nourishment for a medical system glutted on technology, individualism, profit and the pursuit of longevity. Read and be fed."

—Christopher Koller, Health Insurance Commissioner, The State of Rhode Island, USA.

"Unique. Surprising. A real eye-opener. Just about everyone who doesn't have a vested financial interest in maintaining the status quo will agree that U.S. healthcare is badly broken. [This book] is making it possible for us to refocus from how to provide healthcare to how to achieve health. Their description of health as successful functioning in community, rather than as a measure of longevity is a definition that can make a reader feel healthier as they take gradually appreciate the power of the concept. On this foundation, it is not as hard as one might think to outline a healthcare system that is equitable, affordable and achievable."

—Alexander Blount EdD, Professor of Family Medicine, University of Massacusetts Medical Center.